Better Now Than Forever

A Sapphic Fiction Romance

Shelley Tan

Shelley Tan

Contents

Chapter 1

Char loved Dr. Dreamy, a.k.a., Dr. Kelley. Kent. His name was Kent. There had really only been one love in her life, and now there were two. Horses were her first, Kent would be her second. The dates that had happened in Newport and Balboa Island had been incredible. The entire story, in fact, had all of the trappings of a movie, or perhaps a comedic reality show. The way that she had bumped into Dr. Kelley in the hospital and fell down chasing Valerie's dog. The fact that he thought she was homeless with the way she appeared after a workout, sweaty, unshowered, unkempt, and running from security, had endeared her to him. It had been quite a surprise when Kent had asked her out, let alone asked her to marry him. It had been a whirlwind romance but it felt right. There was no need to plan a huge wedding since the Covid pandemic was in full swing, so a quick trip to the courthouse was all it took for her to become Mrs. Char Kelley. Simple and easy, just like life was supposed to be.

Valerie hadn't taken the news very well when Char announced they were moving to northern California. But Kent had an opportunity to transfer, and the lifestyle that Char had dreamed of, one that included horses, was more affordable up north. Char promised Valerie they would stay in touch, and she meant it. In the meantime, Char was happily enjoying her new life, free from the financial constraints and pressure to work that she had had before marrying Kent. She felt like the luckiest girl in the world. And now, instead of having to work, she was able to concentrate on the one thing she had always wanted to do.

There was only one other thing that Char had ever wanted to do, and it was to follow in her mother's footsteps and ride horses. Her mother had been a horse trainer in Santa Barbara and had left Char quite a hefty sum when she had passed, even though she herself had struggled financially. The money had come from an inheritance after her mother had passed, with several acres of land that was quite valuable in Santa Barbara. Her mother's own horse training business had never exactly flourished, but Char was drawn to horses in spite of this. Having grown up around the horses, the atmosphere had been intoxicating to Char as a youngster, but she'd never had the time or money to spend on it. Furthermore, even though her own mother had managed to eke out a career from it, she never wanted Char to follow in her footsteps. Her mother had been hurt, many times, both physically and financially by the horses. She wanted her daughter to do something more "traditional," something where she wouldn't end up hurt and likely destitute, as she had come close to being several times. If only her mother could get her own greedy hands on her daughter's inheritance...but fortunately that wasn't how the will had been set up. Besides, her mother was always wrought with worry. It was no wonder Char had had her first panic attack well before she had even entered adulthood, another trait her mom had unfortunately passed down to her.

But now everything was different! The world wasn't to be afraid of, and she was married to a successful doctor and had moved out of her childhood house years ago. She was happily married and could make her own decisions. And although she seemingly had everything she could ever want, she still had this internal longing that she couldn't explain, that could only be satisfied by being with the horses. This is precisely why, not long after marrying Dr. Kent Kelley, she had sold her home on Balboa and moved north where she could afford to have a decent house and still have enough money left over to dedicate herself to her riding without having to worry about finances. Not that she couldn't afford her small bungalow on Balboa. But affording horses on top of that expense? Even on a doctor's salary, Kent couldn't afford that. He had been kind enough to agree to transfer to a hospital up north where his paycheck would stretch farther.

The horses were healing for her. Her anxiety had gotten so bad over the years that it was difficult for her to do many things. But when she was with the horses, the world stopped. The horses, caring for them, bathing them, and riding them was so consuming that all her worries melted away. She was fortunate to have such a supportive husband and to be surrounded by like-minded people at the barn, who also felt the same way as she did. They understood what she saw, revered almost, about these animals that she had seemed to obsess about since childhood.

There had been a time when Char had lived down south, before she'd received her inheritance, that she had reluctantly given up riding due to her lack of time and financial constraints. Instead, she had tried to focus her energy on working out and getting into shape. Unfortunately, that never really panned out, as her friend and trainer, Valerie, had gotten ill and so their training was thwarted before it ever got off the ground. Never mind that anyway.

She knew from the start that she had been fortunate to marry a doctor, never having to work or focus on money. And the fact that she finally did receive her lofty inheritance not long after her marriage didn't hurt matters in the finance department either. The horses she surrounded herself with were show horses, worth tens of thousands of dollars. And honestly, the initial investment in purchasing the horse was the least of the financial obligations. It was the monthly expenses that prohibited many people from having them. Food, vet bills, supplements, tack, equipment...boarding! Boarding in itself equaled a small car payment. And then, there was the car payment! Meaning, that being on the show circuit and traveling around meant you had to have a way to transport your horse. The only way to do that was with a big truck with a tow package, at least an F250, and a trailer to haul your horse plus sleeping quarters so you could keep a close eye. Char had grown up cared for and sheltered, and even though she resented her parents for protecting her so much, she was also fortunate in that she never had to worry about a roof over her head, even if she didn't have the extra money needed for the horses she so desperately desired. Fortunately, by the time she married a doctor and needed the money, it was there. She never considered her sport to be the elitist sport that it was, as her marriage continued the lifestyle for her that she had grown accustomed to.

Char said goodbye to her husband that morning as she always did and drove the 20 minutes to the stable like she did every morning. It was close to 8 a.m. by the time she left her house, and Kent had already left for work before 7 a.m. It was a cold December day, and so she had on her long blue parka, her Ariat boots lined with faux fur, an apple in her pocket, and a thermos of hot liquid -- watery coffee mixed with cocoa. On her head, she wore a dark wool beanie. It was just above freezing in northern California this time of year, and as Char drove up to Blue Ribbon Stables first thing that morning, she breathed a sigh as she parked her car in front of the large chain-link gate, motor running, so she could pull through. She did not want to have to step out of her warm car into that frigid and damp air. However, seeing as she was at a horse stable, it was necessary to have the gate present in order to prevent any loose horses from leaving the stable. Reluctantly, she climbed out of her warm car, opened the gate, and pulled through into the stable. She then repeated the action in reverse, being sure to secure the gate behind her.

As she walked into the barn, Jose, who lived in a single-wide trailer behind the barn, was just finishing up cleaning out the stalls and was now on to throwing the appropriate ratio of timothy grass to alfalfa hay into each stall. The lights were on in the barn, which contrasted with the gray tule fog that hung low in the air, and a small portable radio was playing some music in Spanish.

"Buenos dias," Char said as she passed Jose.

"Good morning," he responded, reaching for his sombrero and giving her a nod of respect. "How are you today?" he said, with a thick accent.

"Muy, muy, bueno!" Char replied in her best Spanish.

It was cozy and quiet in the barn as the horses all munched contentedly on their hay, the pitter-patter of rain sounding on the tin metal roof overhead. At one end of the barn, a horse was in the cross ties, about to be groomed, and pawing impatiently at the ground.

"Aye!" Char yelled at him, "Knock it off, Di Maggio!" she yelled. "Stop it!" Just then, Kim came out of the tack room with freshly laundered white leg wraps and greeted Char.

"I thought I heard someone out here!" she said cheerfully. "Hey Maggio, cut it out!" she shouted. "Stop pawing! He's so hyper with this rain and cold," Kim said, "perhaps I ought to turn him out before I ride him today."

"Yeah," Char said, looking down the middle of the aisle at Di Maggio, still pawing and now bobbing his head around as much as he could with the cross ties attached to his halter on either side. "That probably wouldn't be a bad idea."

Kim continued to put the pristine white padded leg wraps around each of Di Maggio's fetlocks, making sure he wouldn't accidentally nick himself when he was turned out in the covered arena as he ran around and jumped and rolled and otherwise ran amok. Char looked at Kim again and admired not only her beauty but her life in general. Kim had a super short boy haircut, but that dark hair and eyes, perfect body, and big chest definitely didn't confuse anyone. She was always dressed to the nines, and even today, when it was super cold outside, she looked like she had just stepped out of Equestrian Magazine in her polished black boots, tan breeches, and crisp white polo shirt that was tucked in with a matching black belt. Although she was tall, perhaps five feet, eight or nine inches, she couldn't have been any bigger than a size 4 or 6, and what she didn't bring into the world naturally she had purchased, which was her ample bosom.

All the power to her! Char thought as she wondered if she would ever have the courage to do the same. She had always hated her flat chest, and wearing those padded bras just didn't make her feel any better.

Within minutes Kim was leading Di Maggio, who was big-boned, muscular, and statuesque, down the central aisle of the barn and out toward the covered arena. As she passed by the stalls of the horses who were just finishing up breakfast, a few with food issues pinned their ears and tried to nip Di Maggio as he walked by. Kim was ahead and missed this interaction, so Char stepped in on Kim's behalf.

"Knock it off, Stella!" she grumbled loudly. "Cut it out!" The threat to her food now gone, Stella put her head back down and resumed munching on her breakfast peacefully, and the barn was quiet once again except for the chewing and munching of hay.

Blue Ribbon Stables was absolutely stunning, and that wasn't lost on Char, even on this otherwise gloomy winter day. The barn where she was, unsurprisingly, was painted blue. It was large enough to house 20 horses, with 10 stalls flanking either side of the central aisle. The end of the barn was the lowest part of the property, and as one looked up towards the entrance, you could see the covered arena with the matching blue house behind it, upon the top of the hill. The residents of the house, Joe and Sue Harrison had a view of the entire spread below them. Because the arena was constructed as a pole barn, they could enjoy the view of the riders below even from their house. On hot days, they would invite a few of the girls from the vaulting club to cool off in their pool that was located near the house. As Joe was retired, he spent his days maintaining the grounds, and the grass, trees, and flowers always added to the beautiful park-like setting.

As Kim walked back in from turning out her horse, Char made easy conversation, as the two had become great friends. "How's Jim doing?" Char asked. "And the business? I still need to get down there, Kent and I are looking for some investment opportunities," she said.

"Yeah, yeah...great!" Kim beamed, as she hoisted the black leather saddle out of its zippered bag. "Really good. I'm telling you, Char, the sooner the better. Jim believes with 50 thousand to invest, you and Kent can be well on your way towards retirement within 10 years," she said. "You ought to get in now while the return is still so high..."

"No kidding!" Char responded. "I'll talk to Kent about it tonight. I promise! We will make an appointment...soon!"

Kim and her husband Jim owned an investment firm in the north part of town. By the looks of it, they were doing really well. Kim drove the newest model black Mercedes to the barn, and the two of them lived in a huge 4,000-square-foot house in a newly constructed development with a gate and security. While Kim technically helped out at the firm, between her horses and her own needs, there was little time left over to actually spend at the office. It was fortunate that her husband was just happy to keep his wife so content.

"What about you and Kent?" Kim asked as she carried the saddleback out to the covered arena, pausing before running out into the rain.

"Oh, you know, we're fine. He has his thing and I have mine, but we're good!"

"Okay," Kim yelled back as she ventured toward the covered arena, raindrops pummeling her backside as she hunched forward, trying to protect the expensive saddle from the elements.

As Kim mounted Di Maggio and began her warmup for the day, Char continued to work inside the barn where it was dry, gathering all of her tack for the upcoming ride. She grabbed her brushes, hoof pick, comb, fly spray, reins, and saddle. Check. Check. Check. Check. Check. And that was just for the horse. She then set about gathering the rest of the equipment she'd need for herself -- hard hat, check. Spurs, check. Whip, check. Half chaps, check, and gloves, check. She would carry her water out with her for when she got thirsty. It had always irritated her how non-horse people assumed that the horse did all the work. If that was true, then why was it that everyone who ever went on a horse ride came back and could barely walk for a few days? There was a reason that riding was an Olympic sport, after all. Char was proud of her athleticism and the fact that she could ride these powerful animals.

As was usual with barn and horse etiquette, Char mounted her horse in the center of the arena so as to not interfere with the training that Kim had begun. She warmed up her horse, Mystic, in small circles, loosening his back, his legs, and stretching his neck. She needed her horse supple and engaged. It took extra time in this cold weather. As she continued to walk Mystic around in circles, first in one direction and then the other, Kim began to make polite conversation.

"So did you hear? Sounds like the Harrisons have finally found a trainer! From Germany! She should be arriving here in the next couple of weeks."

"Are you serious? That's fabulous!" Char practically squealed with delight, as her imagination ran wild. She had been dreaming about this day forever, when she could have her very own trainer at the barn, to help her get to the best levels that would be possible for her in her riding "career."

"Who is it?" Char wanted to know. "Tell me everything! What do you know about him, or is it a her? What's their experience? I'm dying! From Germany, really? I hope they stay!"

Although Char was just warming up with Mystic, Kim was well into her training by now and had lost focus on the conversation. Instead, she was trying to get her horse to engage from the hindquarters. It took a few moments before she was able to turn her attention back to Char.

"Um, yeah, her name is Petra. She's from Hamburg. She sent a video over to Joe and Sue. They thought she was good. Apparently, she has won a bunch of awards. I guess she has committed to staying here for a year. If things go well...who knows, could be longer."

"That's fantastic!" Char replied jubilantly. By now Mystic was warmed up and feeling a little frisky himself with the weather. Char thought it better to let all four of them (horses included) return their focus to their training. Surely they could debrief on the details later.

For the rest of the ride, Kim and Char took their horses through their paces, working at an engaged walk, extended trot, and finally a canter in both directions. It was important to perfect their 10-meter circles and all of the basics before moving on to the more advanced maneuvers. After about 45 minutes, Mystic was working nicely under the saddle by pushing from the back end, engaging his back, and reaching for the bit. Char decided that was all for today, and she would reward him with a long rein while she allowed him to walk around until his breathing returned to normal.

Since Kim had begun riding Di Maggio first, she had also ended her workout first and didn't want to waste any time out in the cold in case Di Maggio got too cold. She took him back into the warm barn, dried him off with a damp towel before returning him back to his stall, and checked to make sure the bedding of shavings was fresh. After taking care of Di Maggio first, she then began cleaning off her equipment, sorting the saddle pad, girth and leg wraps in one pile to take home and wash while cleaning the leather bridle and saddle in the tack room before putting them away.

On the way out, Kim poured some grain into the stall with Di Maggio, and his neighing let her know it was a sign of much approval. Kim was already in her Mercedes and heading back out again by the time Char came in from the covered arena. She was disappointed that she hadn't had an opportunity to learn more about the new trainer, Petra, was it? From Germany.

"Oh well," she said quietly as she gently withdrew the bridle from Mystic's mouth, being careful not to let the metal bit bump against his teeth. "We will just have to get the rest of the details another time." Char then briefly thought about stopping by Joe and Sue's up at the house on the way out, but then thought better of it. Although they were incredibly gracious, Char knew that this was their business as well as their residence, and she didn't want to impose on their privacy. Although she was dying to learn more, she would just have to wait.

Chapter 2

Char was serving her husband dinner, scalloped potatoes, salad, and baked chicken when he had finally finished telling her about his day. He was in the middle of a heavy load at work, and it was taking a lot out of him, and she knew she needed to be patient. When he finally finished sharing how his afternoon had wrapped up at the hospital downtown, he asked, "So what about you? Did you go out to the barn today in this weather?"

All Char had to do was to look over at her husband with a smile, and he already knew the answer. "Of course you did…" he answered his own question for himself.

"I thought doctors were relatively smart?" Char teased him.

"Yeah, I suppose you're right," Kent conceded. "Chalk it up to a long day, I guess."

Char told Kent the good news about the trainer from Germany coming. She wasn't sure when, how much her training would cost, or how many lessons she'd be required to take each week. Kent just smiled at his wife, happy that he had the financial means to support her, regardless of the price tag.

"Well, I will say I am relieved it is a woman coming, and not some good-looking single guy that you'll be spending all of this time with. I may be a bit jealous otherwise," he admitted.

"But let me ask you something, dear." Char knew him well enough to know that he was already thinking about this practically. "How is she going to be able to stay in this country? Visas are only good for six months at the most, and the chance of her getting it renewed a bunch of times, well, I just don't see that being very likely. I wouldn't get too attached if I were you."

Char let out a long sigh. *Leave it to Kent to instantly hone in on some sort of negativity,* she mused. "I don't know," she said quickly, annoyed by the question. Couldn't he just let her have this happiness, be excited, unfettered, for just a bit longer? She turned her back as she began to clear the table, the water running in the sink, which meant the conversation was over now. It was too hard to hear, and besides that, she was done. She was glad to have the dishes to tend to, where she could mentally escape back to the barn undisturbed. She couldn't help her irritation, as the new trainer hadn't even arrived yet, and Kent was already making issues about how she'd be able to stay...

Chapter 3

It was another week or two of driving out to ride Mystic before there was any more mention of Petra. Char looked optimistically for her each time she drove out to Blue Ribbon, hoping to see an unfamiliar car, telling her that her new European trainer had finally arrived from Germany. Although she couldn't stand to be away from the barn for more than a day or two, the damp and cold weather of Sacramento was beginning to get old. Char thought about how early she had to come out in the summer to beat the heat, and at the present moment, she wasn't sure which of the two weather conditions she would rather have to contend with. If Char didn't have so many layers of clothing on, she might have seen her tanned, leathery skin which had been permanently damaged from all of the time she had spent in the hot sun. Similarly, her own doctor told her that her lungs looked black, "like a smoker," he'd observed, even though she had never smoked a day in her life. Standing in the dust and dirt of the arena day after day and year after year had taken its toll, as she had spent countless hours inhaling the dust from being out at the barn. She wondered if this is why her "weak spot" seemed to be her lungs, as she was particularly susceptible to chest colds and pneumonia, more so than any other physical ailment.

On my way out of the stable today, she thought, *I'm going to go up to the house and give Joe and Sue the small gift I got them for Christmas, and perhaps I can find out more about when Petra is coming.* As she and the Harrisons regularly exchanged gifts at Christmas, it didn't seem to be too much of a stretch for her to pop in unannounced at this time of the year anyway.

Char could hear the two dogs barking and running in circles behind the door as she waited for it to be opened. The two Australian shepherds, Bella and Luna, were all the security that the Harrisons needed, even with all of the expensive horses down below. Joe opened the door first with a big hearty hello and hug and promptly gave Char a kiss on the cheek, as he had always been accustomed to doing. "Come in, come in! Char! So nice to see you, Char!" he said, turning to call for his wife, "Sue! Sue! We have company! Char's here!" he called cheerfully, simultaneously pushing the dogs away from Char. "Bella! Luna! Behave...go lie down!" he commanded. He reached into his pants pockets, pulled out two small, hard bone-shaped treats, and threw each into the living room where Bella and Luna had been sleeping on their dog beds. The inside of the house was dark on this cold and dreary day, but it didn't feel gloomy. There was a Christmas tree lit in the corner, and on the other side of the living room was a big fireplace, with wood blazing and several logs snapping and sizzling as they turned the living room into the warmest in the house. By now Bella and Luna had returned to their beds in front of the fireplace and were happily finishing the last of their unexpected treat. They quickly settled back down in front of the fire and had already forgotten about Char.

"Char!" Sue said with a smile, rushing toward her with outstretched hands, wearing a white apron down her front. Her hands were covered with flour, and she gave Char a warm embrace while keeping her hands pointed away, not wanting to get flour all over her.

"It's okay," Char said with a laugh, "I just got done riding, so I'm covered in dirt, horse manure, and everything else. In fact, perhaps I should just stand so I don't get your beautiful house dirty."

"Don't be silly," Sue said, waving Char off. "Of course, we don't care about that! We practically live in the barn too," she said. "Isn't that right, Joe?" she asked.

By now Joe was already settled back next to the fire in his big comfy chair, a wood pipe in his right hand, and a glass of whisky sitting next to him. He was holding up the paper and absentmindedly answering Sue at the same time.

"What's that you say?... Ah, yes dear," he said, nodding as he put down his pipe and reached for a sip of his whisky. The fire continued to crackle. The baking from inside the kitchen was becoming more and more noticeable, with wafts of sugar and molasses spilling into the room.

Before Char could even bring it up, Sue was already sharing the good news.

"Did you hear?" she said. "Did you hear? We have a trainer, Petra! From Germany!" She's coming on the first of the year! I can't wait! It will be perfect to get us in shape for spring, and possibly the Dressage Championships this year! I hear they are going to be in San Diego again...how about that? What do you think?"

Sue was clearly just as excited about the news as Char had been, and was sharing all of the exciting news before Char even had to ask.

"Yes, yes! This is just fantastic!" Char agreed. "I can't wait! But where will she stay?" Char wanted to know.

"Well, with us, of course!" Sue replied. "Where else? I mean, she doesn't know anyone, it is a full-time job, you know, and as you are aware, Joe and I have that extra small bedroom with a separate entrance right downstairs. She will be able to come and go as she pleases, without even waking us here in the house! Of course, if she wants to come up and socialize we won't mind," Sue said, "but that will be up to her."

Char nodded, processing it all, and trying to take it all in. "What about her family? Is she married? Does she have anyone?"

"I don't know for sure," Sue replied, "but I am assuming that she isn't married, at least I don't think so, since that would mean she would have to be separated for at least a year. But I hear she does have a sister, Ana, who might come out in the spring. Her sister is excited about getting to come to the US!"

"Well, this is just fantastic!" Char beamed. "We should have a welcome party or something for her once she gets settled. It would be so much fun! I certainly hope she turns out to be a good fit for our little barn."

"Me too," Sue agreed.

"Oh, I almost forgot," Char looked down at the gift she was holding, still in her hand. "Here," she said. "This is for you! Merry Christmas!"

Sue took the present from Char and admired the little wrapped box. Inside was a beautiful ornament of a horse, made of pewter, in the midst of an upper-level dressage movement. It was tied with a little blue ribbon.

Sue's eyes sparkled as she lifted the small figurine into the air for her husband to see.

"Look, honey!" she said. "Look what Char got us for Christmas! It's perfect!" she exclaimed as she walked over to the tree and placed the ornament up top. "I absolutely love it."

"And I absolutely *LOVE* that our barn is going to have its very own trainer!" Char grinned. "No more having to trailer over to other stables just to get some decent lessons!" Char reminded everyone. Bella and Luna looked up at Char as if acknowledging her point, and then promptly lowered their heads on their dog beds and fell back to sleep.

"Merry Christmas!" Char shared as she said goodbye to both Sue and Joe. She raced back to her car and cranked up the heat. She switched gears as she pondered what to make for dinner for her husband as she drove home. In this weather, she reasoned, surely it would be something warm. She struggled to focus on what to make as she drove home, as her mind kept reverting back to the good news of what was to come in the new year at Blue Ribbon.

Chapter 4

har wasn't sure what it was. Sex had never been a huge deal for her, even when she was first married, but at least she had enjoyed it. Lately, she couldn't understand what was going on, but she just wasn't all that interested. She would never tell her husband this, of course, but she really did enjoy being out with the horses a lot more than being intimate with her husband. This realization made her feel terrible, as she loved her husband and he took such good care of her. As he rolled over in bed and began to caress the small of her back with his hand, her decision had already been made. She would do it. Not that she was in the mood, but if she waited until she was in the mood, it might cause an argument, and besides, she didn't want to hurt his feelings. Particularly when she owed all her happiness, her pampered lifestyle, not having to work, and the best part, getting to spend each day at the barn, to him. In addition to cooking dinner for him each night and keeping a tidy house, she had been raised by her mother to tend to her husband's needs whether she felt like it or not. This was never expressly said as such things were not talked about, but Char could infer. When her mother had raised her to be a "proper wife," doing laundry and cooking and whatnot, she was smart enough to figure it all out, whether it was told to her directly or not.

Char had been with her husband long enough to know exactly how their "interlude," so to speak, would play out. First, he would gently touch the small of her back, rubbing her there in circles a few times before letting his hands reach to the top of her panties. Then he would slide them down, and she would roll over to face him, knowing what was coming next. He would kiss her gently on her mouth before inserting his tongue, a metaphor for what would come later. By this time in their marriage, he knew that this wouldn't allow her to get wet on her own, but this didn't seem to bother or deter him. One would suppose this information would incentivize him to try harder at foreplay, but it seemed he took the easy way out, which was to reach for the tube of lubricant in his nightstand and slather it over her privates instead. She tried not to be resentful and didn't know how to ask for this simple request when he was already giving her so much. At this point, he would gently push her knees open and insert himself slowly into her. She laid there and rubbed his back or held his hair, as she loved him, but still, felt nothing. She would wait for it to be over, willing herself to enjoy it, but found it difficult. Her mind would wander, she wondered if this was typical, or better yet, she would start planning the next day in her mind, when she could escape to the place she loved so much. On occasion, she would grab her vibrator so she could enjoy herself too...

When he was done, she would have to get up and clean herself up in the bathroom. By the time she got back, he was often asleep, having satisfied himself from a long and exhausting day.

Chapter 5

The holidays came and went in the usual way, with Kent's parents visiting from Oregon. Since her mom had passed several years ago, Char didn't have a lot of family around except for her younger brother Bill. Occasionally her brother Bill would drive down on his way to Mexico for the rest of the winter, as he was an avid windsurfer, and December through March was the prime time to go. The house had looked beautiful, as always, as Char had always fulfilled her "womanly" duties both inside and outside the bedroom. Char enjoyed the holidays for the most part, but found the endless shopping, decorating, cooking, baking, and wrapping to be exhausting. It was fun to get to see everyone, and she had always gotten along with Kent's parents. However, all of this certainly took away from her time at the stables, and she was anxious to get back there, even if she didn't say it out loud.

Adding to her desire was the urge to impress the new gal, Petra, with her riding. It didn't take long for her horse (or her for that matter!) to lose muscle tone, and after being away from the barn for several weeks she knew she would have some catching up to do. She didn't want Petra to think she had come all the way from Germany for some second-rate stable. Blue Ribbon had a good reputation despite not having its own trainer, and Char was hoping that having Petra here would give the barn the added boost it needed to become the best around. More importantly, Char wanted to be the best. She hoped Petra would be her ticket. *If that was so*, she told herself, *I had better get cracking.*

New Year's Eve had been spent at the annual New Year's party with the other doctors that Kent worked with. A beautiful modern building with staircases, chandeliers, and high ceilings had been rented out for the affair, and as usual, Char felt compelled to wear something new. When she walked out into the foyer of her house as they prepared to leave, Kent gave her the once over and clearly liked what he saw. She was wearing a solid red gown that was off the shoulder on one side, held up by the tiniest of straps. The other side was solid, and the tight-fitting dress skimmed her body down to the calves where it ended in flouncy ruffles. She had matching red stilettos and wore exquisite red rubies on her ears and neck. She truly was a vision, and she knew it.

"Wow," was all Kent could muster as his eyes ran the length of her up and down. He lifted his right hand in a circular motion as if to say "turn around."

Char did as she was asked and spun around for him once so that he could see her fully. She enjoyed the positive attention. Kent then looked at his watch, as if trying to see if they had time for a quick romp.

"No!" Char said firmly, this time not feeling the slightest bit guilty. "Do you know how long it has taken me to put myself together? One quick romp with you and it will all be ruined, mister! The hair, the makeup...the dress will be wrinkled...absolutely not!"

"Okay, okay," Kent stopped her, motioning toward the door. "Then let's make it an early night," he said, adjusting himself.

Char and Kent got in the car and drove downtown to where the party was being held. All of the other doctors and hospital staff were there, along with their wives, and a few with girlfriends or fiancees. Everyone looked stunning. Char felt her anxiety approaching, and turned to Kent, "I am going to get a glass of champagne. Would you like one?" she smiled.

"Absofuckinglutely!" he whispered, nibbling on her ear as he said it. Well, she certainly knew one thing was on his mind anyway. *Perhaps too many of these and he won't be able to perform later,* she thought devilishly to herself.

"Here you are, honey," she said sweetly, handing him a glass of champagne. Kent was already hobnobbing with several of his colleagues from the hospital, and they welcomed Char graciously into their little circle when she approached.

The atmosphere of the party was absolutely stunning. There were 30-foot-tall Christmas trees; Char must have counted five or six in the room. Each one was decorated with a different theme -- all gold with gold ornaments, a gold star, and gold beads. One was done with crimson bows, red lights, and matching little red bells of all sizes. The tree by the door had ornaments with the hospital's logo, and little sparkling silver ornament wreaths to take home as a souvenir.

The classical Christmas music was being performed live by a local jazz band, and many couples were already dancing under the lights that hung down from the ceiling of the large hall. It was absolutely breathtaking. Char felt her anxiety begin to fade as the bubbles hit her stomach. One glass took the edge off, but a second glass would really help her relax. Char waited for an appropriate time to interrupt the conversation before asking the group if she could get anyone another round.

"I'll take one, thanks, Char," replied the pretty blonde standing to the right of her husband.

"No problem," Char responded. "Anybody else? Can I grab one for anyone else while I'm getting more?"

The little group was just then further interrupted by a waiter who came by offering a plate of absolutely scrumptious-looking hors d'oeuvres: mini cheese and spinach puffs in phyllo dough, a variety of sushi rolls, gourmet cookies, and bites of cheesecake. Char could feel her dress clinging tighter to her stomach and abdominal area just thinking about all these wonderful delectables. She found it comforting that she would absolutely be riding in the morning, hopefully burning off these extra calories before they had a chance to turn into fat.

The rest of the evening carried on in much the same fashion, with dancing, tasting, sipping, and hobnobbing with all of the colleagues from the hospital. By 11 p.m., Char and Kent had had enough and said their farewells. They said goodbye and got in their car to drive the few minutes back to their house. Fifteen minutes later Char and Kent had safely arrived back home. By 11:20 p.m., Char had fallen into bed and was soon fast asleep, already dreaming of her day ahead that would be spent at the barn, her favorite place to be.

The next morning Char awoke at 7 a.m. with a dull headache from the champagne that she'd imbibed the night before. She quickly popped two Tylenol into her mouth and was about to hit the shower when she thought better of it. She could see her husband's side of the bed was empty and she could hear the water running in the bathroom, so she knew he had beat her to the shower. Not wanting to wait around and waste extra time, Char shrugged her shoulders and changed gears. Instead, she opened up her dresser that was full of riding breeches and pulled out her loosest pair, not wanting to have to squeeze into something ill-fitting, especially after last evening's indulgences. She grabbed a riding shirt and sweatshirt and headed to the kitchen to pack a few things before heading out. Just as she was about to head out to the car, her husband came into the kitchen freshly showered and gave her a hug and a kiss before heading out for the day. The smell of his fresh-smelling face and cologne mixed to remind her of freshly cut grass in spring.

"Mmmmm..." she breathed him in. She laughed at the thought of how she'd smell after being at the barn, in contrast to Kent's fresh scent.

"Have a great day, hon," he said as he opened the door to the garage. "I'll see you tonight."

"Right behind you!" Char echoed as she followed behind. Within seconds both Char and Kent had gone, leaving both the house as well as the holidays behind.

Chapter 6

As was usual, Char stopped her car in front of the gate and got out in the freezing cold air to manually open it before driving through and closing it behind her. She was focused on how cold she was, and how she hated getting out of her cozy car to complete this irritating ritual each morning when she almost ran into the new car in her usual parking spot.

Was this a new boarder? she wondered. She knew that the Harrisons didn't have a full barn and had advertised a few "specials" to try and get more boarders in for the new year. More boarders meant more money for the Harrisons, and Char certainly understood that. Char readjusted her parking spot, turned off the heavenly heat that was now blasting at her face and feet, and reluctantly left her warm car. The new boarder was already riding in the arena, and Char could tell instantly that she had a lot of experience. She was gracefully executing upper-level movements such as piaffe and flying lead changes every other stride. Char stopped in her tracks to watch this beautiful display before it hit her that this must be Petra!

Not wanting to interrupt, Char dropped her belongings at her feet and stood quietly at the edge of the arena, watching with admiration. She thought about the Harrisons, and agreed instantly that they had been right! They really picked an expert rider. By the looks of it, Petra was easily riding the grand pre-level of dressage. Her insides were doing cartwheels as she watched the amazing maneuvers being performed, not at some Olympic competition, but right here in front of her on her own home turf! She wanted to pinch herself or blink, but all she could do was stand there quietly, barely breathing, in complete and total adulation. This was who and what she'd always wanted to be. It was her, only it wasn't. Too her, it was everything.

Char didn't know how long she had been standing at the railing, watching Petra, who hadn't yet noticed Char, before she realized how cold she was. She hadn't been aware of anything other than the brilliance and beauty before her until suddenly her hands were burning from the cold and she came to and realized she was shaking from head to toe. Ordinarily, Char couldn't wait to get on her horse, Mystic, and ride. But today, she didn't know what to do, as she didn't want to miss a second of what was unfolding right in front of her. Char increasingly felt the cold biting at her and willing her to go inside to get warm, but her eyes were so riveted that she stood still, watching until she could bear it no more. She had no idea how much time had elapsed before she finally and reluctantly bent over slowly, eyes still on Petra, and picked up her belongings. She walked slowly into the barn only so that she wouldn't get frostbite on her limbs.

Once inside the barn, Char remained dazed from either the cold or disbelief that she hadn't been dreaming. She went through the motions of getting Mystic ready to ride, all the while wishing that she was still outside watching Petra. The only way to get to witness more of this was to get Mystic ready as fast as she could, and begin her own riding out in the arena where she would be warm. Then she would be able to catch glances of Petra riding without freezing to death in the meantime. The riding workout was so intense that often Char would have to strip layers off of herself as she rode, casting the articles of clothing such as a jacket or sweatshirt onto the side railings as she strode along. Same for the horses. At the end of a training session, even on these coldest of days, the horses would be wet from sweat after the ride. Just like their human counterparts, it would be necessary to dry them and put a blanket back on them before their body temperature lowered as they came down from their workout so that they too didn't become chilled and get sick.

Fortunately for Char, Petra was still in the arena riding as Char walked Mystic into one end of the arena to lunge him before her ride.

"Mind if I lunge my horse on this end for a few?" Char called out to Petra. Although Char had mixed German and Scottish heritage herself, she hadn't known too many people who had been from Germany. All of her family had emigrated to the United States generations ago. Upon first glance, Petra appeared much as Char would have expected, with an athletic build, albeit more stocky than she would have imagined, and approximately the same height, five feet five inches, as Char. Petra was wearing quite a few layers, but Char was able to make out sparkling blue eyes with blonde curls that framed Petra's face. Char couldn't be sure if it was a smile or not that had appeared on Petra's face as she slowed her horse down to a walk, and turned towards Char at the other end of the arena.

Char panicked, horrified at having interrupted the brilliant workout that Petra had been working on. *Great,* she thought to herself. *We haven't even exchanged names yet and I've already pissed her off.* Although Char had no way of knowing for sure, she had heard that some of these European trainers who came over to the States were pretty full of themselves. She hoped that she and Petra weren't already off to an uncomfortable start.

Petra walked her horse right up to where Char was standing and stopped.

"Hello," she said, with a thick German accent. "My name is Petra," Petra introduced herself, pronouncing "is" like "ease". Char instantly found this slight imperfection in her pronunciation quite charming. She felt the sudden urge to repeat the foible back but resisted the compulsion. Instead, she introduced herself properly.

"Hi Petra, I'm Char. It is so nice to meet you."

"Thank you," Petra said, still smiling, looking directly at Char and nodding her head with appreciation.

"Um, well gosh, there is so much I want to say to you. You ride beautifully," Char stammered.

Char couldn't believe herself. Wasn't it just last night that she was hanging out with a bunch of well-educated doctors, sharing drinks and laughter without a worry? And now today, she could barely get a word out without feeling like a little kid who had just met their favorite rock star. What was wrong with her? *There goes that darn social anxiety again,* she chided herself before remembering that last night she had had champagne. *Isn't that what they call "liquid courage"?* she mused. *Sure could use some of that right now,* she thought again. She really did feel as though she was standing in front of an idol of some sort, someone she could only dream of becoming someday with enough proper riding instruction under her belt.

"Thank you for the compliment," Petra responded. "Yes, yes, there will be much time for that later, when it isn't so cold. Let's get back on our horses and continue our riding before one of us freezes to death out here, huh? We can get to know each other later when we can go somewhere and talk where it is not so cold."

"Yes, sounds good," Char managed. "Okay then, so I won't bother you by lounging my horse down here?"

"No, not a problem," Petra responded. "Just stay in the center and then I can ride around you if I need to."

Since the arena was of standard size, almost 200 feet in length and 66 feet wide, there was plenty of room for both riders to do what they needed to do without getting in one another's way. Char began as she normally did by warming up Mystic with the circingle, side reins, and lounge line, the lounge whip seldom needed but following close behind Mystic near the ground to encourage proper use and engagement to push forward and not pull himself along lazily. It was critical that the proper muscles were to be working during the warmup.

For the most part, the two ladies concentrated on their individual objectives in the arena, staying out of one another's way. As in any sport, dressage had its rules of etiquette, and both women were seasoned enough to know them well.

This is exactly why it caught Char off-guard when all of a sudden she heard Petra yelling critiques her way. "A leetle more leg...good, good...soften the hand, outside rein...yes! Very good, Char!" she exclaimed enthusiastically. "Very good. You can see the difference in his movement now, eh?"

Char was having too much fun to let her nerves take over. She couldn't believe this! Was she the first one to have an actual lesson with Petra? She couldn't wait to talk to Kim!

Finally, Mystic came to a slow walk, and Char took the opportunity to thank Petra for the pointers.

"No problem!" Petra said after Char had thanked her profusely. "It's why I'm here!"

"Okay," Char replied cautiously, adding, "but I know you came here all the way from Germany. We don't expect you to provide charity to us."

"Don't worry about that for now," Petra assured Char. "We will figure that out another time." And with that, Petra dismounted from her horse and was gone, leading him back to the barn.

Char tried to continue her ride, focusing on the suggestions Petra had mentioned, but too much was swirling in her head. She couldn't wait to tell everyone about her experience and meeting Petra this morning! Instead, she took her time cooling Mystic off, walking around and around, changing directions, changing patterns, until it was clear that Mystic was no longer breathing heavily. The flare of a horse's nostrils was a giveaway as to their breathing, and by the looks of it, Mystic was no longer laboring to breathe. The trick was to get him inside the barn now and dried off before things went too far in the opposite direction and he became chilled.

Once inside the barn, Char looked around for Petra but didn't see her. The horse that she had been riding was tucked away back inside his stall, head leaning out the open upper door to inspect the action inside the barn. Char began to wonder where Petra could have gone when suddenly Petra appeared in the aisle, seeming to have popped out of her horse's stall.

"What's his name?" Char ventured.

"Erde," Petra said, "It means 'earth.'"

"Erde," Char repeated, slowly. "Is that right?"

"Yes," Petra said smiling. "And you? What is your horse's name?"

"This is Mystic," Char said. "It reminds me of the word 'mystical,' which is how I think of horses, you know? They are mysterious, magical, I suppose. Well, at least that's how I think of them," she said.

"Ya, ya," Petra nodded in agreement, still smiling. "Nice horse you have. Have you had him long? My guess is he is perhaps around seven or eight years. Is that so?"

"Actually, he is closer to 10, but yeah. He's not bad," Char said, as she wiped the girth area one last time with a towel and felt afterward for any moisture left under his belly. Satisfied that he was dried off enough to put back in his stall, she began to untie him when Petra asked,

"So...are you interested in taking lessons from me?"

Char tried to contain herself as she was shocked by the boldness and also honored. Taking a lesson from someone like Petra would be, quite frankly, amazing!

"Yes! I would love to!" Char's words were out of her mouth almost before she could stop them. "That would be wonderful!"

"Okay," Petra nodded, eyes still sparkling. "I am not cheap. I will tell you that right now. But if you want to learn to ride like the Germans, I can teach you. We are the best, you know."

"Yeah, sure," Char said, nodding. She knew that ordinarily, money wasn't an issue for her, but exactly how much was Petra expecting?

"And another thing," Petra was already setting the ground rules, "My lessons are one hour. If you are late, or you cancel, there is no refund. I get paid for my time and if I have set aside the time, I get paid no matter what. Understood?"

Nodding once again, Char looked back at Petra, "Yes," she replied, "understood."

"Okey...dokey," Petra said slowly as if trying out these American colloquialisms. She winked. "Did I say that okay?" she asked, a small laugh escaping her.

"Okey dokey, yes," Char repeated for her. "Perfect! Your English is actually quite good."

"Okey dokey!" Petra repeated.

"All right then," Char said, as she watched Petra walk out of the barn, presumably up to the Harrisons' house where her room was. Char called after her. "Nice meeting you!" she yelled. It was too late. By the time she looked up from taking her boots off, Petra had already left the barn and had rounded the corner to head up towards the house. Char simply shrugged her shoulders and finished cleaning her tack, excited for her first lesson.

Chapter 7

I t was after 8 p.m. and Char was just getting ready for bed when her cell
phone rang. She went to reach it and looked down to see who was calling.
It was Sue Harrison, and she sounded really excited.

"Char, hi! I heard you met Petra! What do you think?"

"Hi Sue," Char said, remembering to breathe between each of her own
words. "How are you? Yes, I met Petra today! In fact, she is going to give me my
first lesson tomorrow morning! I am so excited!"

"Oh, how wonderful!" Sue's voice sounded delighted for Char. "I might have
to come on down and take a look at your lesson. You never know, I may learn
something!" Sue teased.

"Yeah, yeah, of course," Char responded. Of course, she wouldn't mind. "So
is that why you're calling?"

"Yes...um, I mean, no. Well, sort of. Yeah, I wanted to see how your initial
meeting with Petra was, and I also wanted to see what you're doing next
Friday night. I'm thinking of having a barn party for Petra, you know, a
get-to-know-you kind of deal, to welcome her. What do you think?"

"Yeah," Char said. "Sounds like fun. What time?"

"Seven. And bring an appetizer if you can, dear. That would be fantastic!"

As the matriarch of Blue Ribbon, Sue often took to treating her boarders
more like her own children than actual clients. Sue, who was older than the
other ladies, didn't try to hide her age. She donned grey hair and was a little
portly. Since she was older, she could get away with such phrases as "dear"
and "honey," and no one seemed to mind. She did so much for everyone at
the stable that no one questioned her when on a rare occasion she asked for a
small favor (such as an appetizer to be brought).

"Of course, I will, Sue! You know you can count on me!"

"I know I can, dear," she said. "See you tomorrow!"

"See you tomorrow," Char echoed back. And with that, Char turned back to the sink to finish her nightly routine.

<h1 style="text-align:center">Chapter 8</h1>

It was a cold January morning when Char awoke. She listened to the trees blow around outside and the rain pound down her downspout outside her bedroom. She flipped over, delving deeper into her soft covers when, she suddenly leaped up out of bed, remembering her first lesson with Petra!

A lazy morning lounging in bed would have to wait. Now that she remembered, it was as if a shot of adrenaline had gone straight to her heart and she was heading towards the kitchen, making coffee and organizing herself for the day. She rushed around at such a frenetic pace that she nearly knocked into Kent as she turned the corner, flying as fast as she could into the kitchen.

"Whoa! Good morning there!" Kent said as he looked behind him, trying not to lose sight of the flurry that had spun past him. "What's the rush?"

"Oh, hey!" she called after him. "Morning! I have my first lesson with Petra this morning, you know, the new trainer from Germany?"

"That's right," Kent was suddenly back in the kitchen, leaning against her and kissing the back of her neck. Char felt a delightful chill where he kissed her, and the hairs on the back of her neck stood on end.

"Mmmmm..." she turned around, kissing him in return on the lips. "Wish me luck today!" She said, as she took her arms and wrapped them tightly around his neck in a huge hug.

"Good luck!" he said. "Love you!" And with that, he was out the door.

"Love you too!"

Char rounded up everything she needed for the day and threw a steaming cup of coffee into her thermos. She pulled her car out of the garage and watched as the rain pummeled the windows. It was coming down so fast and furiously that the wipers could barely keep up. Char backed out of the driveway carefully, going more slowly than she wanted to, as she was so excited to get to the barn that not even this torrential downpour could squelch her enthusiasm. She drove carefully to the barn, not wanting to jinx anything on her first day.

It was about 8:30 a.m. when she arrived at the barn. As usual, she put her car in park and ran over to the gate, hopped back in, and then promptly closed the gate behind her as soon as she was through. She looked over at the covered arena, still dry, thank God, and saw Petra riding Erde. It was absolutely just as breathtaking as the first time she had seen her, but Char knew better than to watch and risk being late for her first lesson. She willed herself away from the dressage movements that Petra was practicing, and forced herself into the barn to get Mystic saddled up and ready.

"Hey, Kim!" Char said when she saw Kim inside the barn with her horse, Di Maggio. "How long have you been here?"

"Right before you," Kim replied.

Just then, Jose passed by with a wheelbarrow full of horse manure from cleaning the stalls. "Morning, Jose!" Char called out to him.

"Well, you seem awfully cheerful today, on this cold and blustery day, Miss Char!" Kim teased.

"Yes, I am!" Char replied. "I have my first lesson today with Petra! I am so excited!"

"Awesome!" Kim beamed back. "I am so excited for you!"

"Thanks!" said Char. "What about you? Are you signed up yet?"

"Yes, mine is actually right after you today!" Kim said. "I'm here early to go lunge Di Maggio a bit, and work out my own nerves," Kim admitted. "I'll be watching your lesson too if you don't mind."

"Not a bit," Char responded cheerfully. "See ya."

"See ya!"

With Jose out dumping the manure, and Kim out of the barn, Char was left alone with nothing but her thoughts. "All right Mystic," she said quietly. "It's just you and me, boy. Are you ready?" Although Char had gone through the same routine thousands of times, she stood still, looking over her horse and her equipment, making sure she hadn't forgotten anything. Satisfied that she had everything she needed, she took one last deep breath and walked Mystic to the end of the barn, where she stopped. There were about 30 feet between the end of the barn and the covered arena, and the rain was unrelenting. Char readied herself for the onslaught, and at the count of three, ran with Mystic right behind her as fast as she could through the rain. She tried not to slip as there were big mud puddles on the ground by now. Mystic jumped over one of the puddles, nearly landing on top of Char.

By the time Char and Mystic made it into the arena, Char's clean tack and well-groomed horse were both splattered in mud.

"Aye!" Petra teased, "Glad you came so prepared for your first lesson! No worries, right? We are going to get dirty out here in the mud anyway, eh?"

Char grinned and walked Mystic over to the mounting block. It wasn't possible to get on Mystic easily since he was over 16 hands, and so Char had become accustomed to using the mounting block to get up.

"Okay, okay," Petra began, her face becoming all business. "You just warm-up, and do your thing. I am going to stand here and watch for a moment, get a feel." Petra stood in the center of the long arena, watching as Char warmed up on 10 and 20-meter circles. Char could see her better this time because Petra had taken off her hat and jacket during her ride, with only her riding breeches and white collared shirt remaining. Petra had a fine appearance, with her shirt tucked into the black breeches and a black belt looped around her pants. Char could see that Petra's face was still red from her ride, and little wisps of sweat separated her blond hair into pieces along her forehead. From atop her horse, Petra appeared shorter in stature than at ground level, but as before she was dressed neatly and professionally, and carried an unmistakable athletic build along with her air of confidence, which Char admired.

The lesson progressed smoothly, although Char's nerves made it difficult to relax. She was tight and tense in her shoulders, stiff with her hands, and found it difficult to sit deeply in the saddle with her buttocks clenched. She knew she could do better, but tried her best to hide her nervousness from Petra.

"It is just so cold out here, I am shivering," she said, attempting to blame her tension on the weather. But both knew better, and Petra wasn't fooled.

"Nah..." she countered. "You are not cold. You are working. Besides, look at all of the layers you have on."

By now, even Mystic was beginning to work up a sweat, as Petra had progressed the lesson to a demonstration of 15-meter circles with serpentines in the middle.

"More flexion through the center!" she commanded. "Come on, Char, one more time. This time I want you to sit the trot as you show me the proper bend."

Char wasn't sure how much time had gone by, but her muscles were so tired by now that she was unable to hold tension in any part of her body anymore. She felt all of her muscles release, and suddenly, with her deeper seat, Mystic began moving better underneath her.

"Yes, Char! Yes! That's it! That's the way...Don't back off now, just a slight squeeze with the inside rein...Yes! Okay, that's good. Now I want you to give him a long rein, and we will talk while you let him cool down. What do you think?"

Char was trying to catch her breath and took several moments before answering with more than a nod. "Yeah," she finally managed, exhausted. "Yeah, that was good. Thank you."

"Okay then. Yes, that was good. Not bad for your first lesson," she said.

Petra then turned to Kim, who had been waiting quietly at the other end of the arena for her lesson. Feeling dismissed, Char continued until Mystic was fully cooled off before dismounting and leading him back to the barn. Although Char usually rode at least four or five days a week, she could feel the muscles in her inner thighs aching as she managed to limp back into the barn to clean up and put Mystic away. With her first lesson under her belt, she finally slowed down both mentally and physically. She was absolutely drained. With the initial excitement and nervousness now behind her, she was ready to collapse. She hopped in her car and left without saying goodbye to Kim or Petra, as she didn't want to interrupt them. She looked forward to getting out of the wet weather and into her warm bed back at home. As tired as she was, she felt accomplished and satisfied. She knew she was on her way.

Chapter 9

It seemed as though the week had flown by. Was tomorrow Friday already? Char still hadn't figured out what to wear to the welcome party for Petra, and if she was going to buy something new, she'd have to hurry up and go get it.

At least the rain has finally let up for the time being, she thought to herself. Not only was tomorrow Friday and she still didn't know what to wear, but she also needed to run to the store and figure out what she was bringing as an appetizer. Meanwhile, Kent had been working late at work all week, and the two had barely passed one another. Char felt guilty as she thought about tomorrow night without her husband. Although he was technically invited to the soiree, it wasn't really his crowd. Most of them were women, except for Joe, and all of them loved horses. When Kent wasn't working or coming home late from the office, he preferred to kick back on the weekends watching football or baseball, or work on some project around the house if he was feeling motivated.

Should I be missing Kent more than this? she asked herself. It's not that she didn't love her husband; she did. It was just that after years of marriage things had become mundane and she had so much in common with her girlfriends at the barn. As someone who spent most of her free time tending to the home and fixing dinner, unlike her husband, her fun took place outside of the house.

At least it certainly took place outside of the bedroom...

That was a topic that Char hoped to kick down the road as far as she could. Why was sex such a big deal to men anyway? She'd read that it was natural for her sex drive to diminish as she aged. At least for a few of her friends that she'd talked to, they had said the same thing. Except of course for Kim and Jim. *Oh, the stories that Kim told!* Char could hardly believe her ears. At work, in the office, at the stable, in the back of the Mercedes...those two were unstoppable! It was amazing that they'd never been caught, although it sounded like there had definitely been some close calls. Calls that would have been far too close for Char to even consider the idea. But she did wonder, what would it be like to be in a relationship where you desired, actually wanted your man, in that way? It was one thing to be wanted, and Char certainly appreciated the positive attention that Kent paid her, but the simple fact was that she just was...she didn't know. *Menopausal? Frigid? Gay, lesbian, or bisexual?* Char actually let out a little laugh as she considered the last three options. Not that she had anything against anyone or their sexual preference. She certainly wasn't a prude or some religious zealot or anything of the sort. She was proud that she considered herself to be open-minded when it came to most things. However, she had just never had any real interest in anyone other than a few boys she'd dated before she was married, and of course her husband, until recently. She just didn't know what it was. *The less I worry about it, the less of a problem it will be,* she kept reassuring herself. Besides, she led a rich life in so many ways. But for some reason, she just couldn't stop the unwanted thoughts that something was missing. She didn't know what it was, but she hoped she'd figure it out, and soon.

Fortunately, Char's unwanted thoughts were interrupted by Kim, who was calling about the party tomorrow night.

"Hey, girl!" Her friend emoted enthusiasm. "You're going tomorrow night, right?"

"Yes, of course!" Char responded, trying to match her friend's enthusiasm. As always, Char had mixed emotions regarding these types of events, as she loved everything to do with horses and horse people, but always found herself anxious at these social events. Maybe she'd ask Kim for a ride so that she could have a glass of wine or two and not have to worry about driving home.

"Do you mind if I get a ride to the party with you tomorrow night?" Char asked.

"Of course not!" Kim said. "But you'll have to squeeze in, Jim is going too."

Of course he is, Char thought, angered by her own envy over Kim's seemingly perfect marriage. As Kent never attended these functions, Char didn't need to explain where he was. Since he never attended anyway, no one even bothered asking where he was anymore. It would have been more unusual if Char announced that he *was* going to the party.

"See you at eight?" Kim confirmed before hanging up the phone.

"Sounds good. See you then!" Char hung up the phone and returned to her former ruminations regarding the perfect appetizer and outfit for tomorrow's big event.

Chapter 10

K im, Jim, and Char could hear the music and laughter coming from the
house before they even made it to the front door.

"Should we knock?" Kim asked. "I seriously doubt anyone will hear us out
here anyway," she said.

Before anyone could answer, Jim, rapped quickly and loudly with the brass
door knocker that hung on the wooden door. The three stood quietly waiting,
staring ahead at the door for about 30 seconds before the door swung wide
open, with a smiling Sue standing behind it. Her arms were outstretched with
a ready embrace for each of them, and the jovial mood inside instantly eased
most of the anxiety that Char had felt about the social gathering.

Most of the anxiety, Char thought as Sue offered her a glass of wine, but there
was always that residual angst that the glass of wine would be sure to eradicate.
She actually felt a little more anxious than usual and thought that it was the
excitement of getting to know Petra.

"Ah, yes!" she responded gratefully to Sue and then quietly to herself, *this
should do it!*

As the three entered the cozy living room, still decorated from the holidays,
they looked around to take it all in. There was quite a crowd there. Most of the
people Char knew, but there were a few that she didn't know. Mostly the few
that she didn't know were women who had to come to ride after work, long
after she'd already left for the day. She'd seen them around occasionally on the
weekends but wasn't well acquainted. And there in the corner was the guest of
honor, Petra.

Petra seemed to be taking everything in stride, looking quite comfortable
with everything: being in a new country, speaking in English, being the focal
point of the attention. She stood immersed in conversation with a small group

of riders facing her, asking her questions about her trip, how she liked California, what brought her here, and so on and so forth.

Not only did Char admire her sense of adventure and riding ability, but Char couldn't help but notice her natural beauty as well. Perhaps it was her confidence and good-natured persona that she projected that had Char's attention. Her short blonde locks framed her face. She didn't wear any makeup and didn't seem to require any anyway. Rather, her smile and blue eyes, and that strong sturdy build made her beautiful in Char's eyes. Char was excited to go and talk to her, as she hadn't since her lesson. She walked over and stood behind the small group of people that were already joined in conversation with Petra, and listened, not wanting to interrupt.

"Hello!" Petra stopped and greeted Char warmly as she did with everyone when Char approached.

"Hi," Char felt both excited and shy, almost as though she was standing in front of a celebrity. In Char's mind, Petra was like a celebrity, as she was from another country and was the type of rider that Char only aspired to be like one day. There was so much that was intriguing about Petra, who Char discovered, was from Hamburg. She had won countless riding awards, spoke two languages...there was just so much to be admired, and Char had hardly even begun to know her. Char thought she was so brave for leaving her native Germany and coming to the States all on her own at a young age.

The rest of the evening was equally pleasant. Sue and Joe had put out a variety of foods for people to help themselves. There were cheeses, a variety of meats, some bean soup and salad, crusty rolls, and a separate table just for desserts. The guests helped themselves and sat around and talked and got to know Petra. There was plenty of wine, beer, and other beverages available. All in all, everyone seemed to have a great time. Although Char didn't really get much of an opportunity to talk to Petra personally with so many people gathered, she did enjoy being part of the group conversation and learning more about Petra.

Petra had a younger sister who was still living in Germany, along with her parents. By the sound of it, her family wasn't rich but certainly wasn't struggling. Petra described them as being quite strict and conservative, which had proven both detrimental as well as positive for Petra growing up. It is also what allowed her to be so independent at a young age. The conversation led to Petra's personal relationships, and she shared that she was single, which had obviously made it much easier for her to come to the States on her own, rather than have an emotional tie holding her back.

The gathering dispelled for the most part around 11 p.m., with Char, Kim, and Jim being one of the last ones to leave. Char thanked Sue and Joe for their hospitality, hugged them each goodbye, and left. Char told Petra she would look forward to seeing her at the barn in the morning, and they confirmed her lesson for 9 am.

That night in bed, Char was trying to fall asleep when she felt Ken's breath on her neck. She stiffened as she realized he was wanting sex. She was still thinking about the party she had attended and how fun it was meeting everyone.

She pictured Petra in the corner of the room, captivating everyone's attention, as she felt Kent's hand reach around her backside and fondle her breast. Her back was to him, and she was momentarily distracted from thinking about the party as his hand on her breast brought her back to reality. As usual, she really was not in the mood tonight, and so continued not to move, hoping he would assume she was asleep and his attempts at sex would be thwarted. She felt his hand caress her breast, as his fingers circled her nipple. Instinctively, her nipple reacted to the touch and hardened, an unwanted response that would only inspire his desires further. Her only option was to otherwise remain still, hoping he would satisfy his desires in other ways so that she could be left alone and get to sleep. She felt bad, but tonight she just was not willing to compromise. She continued to lay as still as possible with her eyes closed and a focus on deep breathing to give the illusion that she was already asleep.

Fortunately, it worked. Within minutes his hand fell back over her shoulder as it left her breast, and she could feel the mattress shift underneath her as he rolled back onto his side of the bed. She relaxed her breathing. The stiffness in her muscles eased and she was able to let her body relax. When she awoke, he was gone. She breathed a sigh of relief and began to ready herself for the day ahead.

Chapter 11

Char stopped her car in front of the gate of Blue Ribbon and got out of the car. Kim pulled up in her black Mercedes and followed her in, saving Char from having to get out and close the gate again. It was a clear January day, but at 9 a.m. it was still only a little over 40 degrees Fahrenheit, and Char could see her breath in front of her, as well as the frost that clung to the tips of the grass in front of the arena.

She zipped up her parka and put her gloves on as she headed for the barn, and greeted Kim. "Morning, Kim!" she called. "How are you today?"

Kim gave her a knowing look, and Char knew exactly what it meant. Kim and Jim had been up late again after the party having sex.

"Let me guess," Char teased. "You're tired, right? Didn't get much sleep last night, I assume?"

Kim just giggled and Char knew she had guessed correctly.

"Not me!" Char bragged. "I went straight to sleep and I am ready to roll this morning. I am sure Kent wasn't thrilled about it, but I just wasn't in the mood."

"Char, you're never in the mood!" Kim told Char. "Poor Kent! You better watch out if you want to keep your pampered lifestyle," she cautioned.

All of a sudden, Char's smile fell from her face and Char realized they were no longer joking around. "What do you mean?" Char asked, not sure if she wanted to hear the response.

"Nothing," Kim said, changing the subject. "Hey, what time is your lesson with Petra today?" Kim was now looking up towards the house and saw Petra in her riding clothes heading towards them.

"Morning ladies," she said cheerfully. "Char, Kim, nice to see you. Fun party last night, eh?" Everyone agreed it had been a nice evening and an opportunity for everyone to get to know one another. "I am surprised to see you all here so early today," she added.

Char couldn't resist the opportunity to take a quick teasing jab back at Kim.

"Yes, well, I should be fine today," Char said, grabbing her things. "But Kim didn't get much sleep last night, I'm sure she'll have a tough time today," she said, as she watched Kim walk away towards the barn.

Kim correctly understood she was being teased and turned back with a retort of her own, as she wasn't exactly ready to share the details of her sex life with someone she had just met.

"I didn't sleep well last night because alcohol does that to me sometimes," she yelled.

Char was still standing next to Petra and asked if she was riding today.

"Of course!" she said. Char liked that Petra always seemed to have a smile on her face, one more thing that she admired about her.

"Okay then, let's go get ready." They headed down into the barn to get their horses ready for the day. Kim, who had headed into the barn a few moments before, had already thrown the halter on Di Maggio and was leading him into the arena to run around and burn off some energy before the arena was occupied. She passed Char and Petra as she exited the barn.

Meanwhile, Char and Petra talked casually in the barn as they readied their horses for the day.

"So how are you adjusting to everything?" Char asked as she used her curry comb to make big swooping circles over Mystic's winter coat.

Petra laughed. "So far, so good," she said, "but I really do need to get off this property for a bit. I haven't seen anything here except horses, and the house and the barn. I don't even know how to get to the grocery store!" She laughed again.

Without a moment's hesitation, Char leapt at the chance to offer to show Petra around. "Well, if you want, I can take you around today and show you where things are." It was out of her mouth before she even thought about Kent. *Shit!* she thought, realizing that Kent had expected her home later this afternoon. It was the weekend, and weekends were generally the only time that she and Kent had to spend any quality time together. She quickly dismissed the thought. She would figure something out. Kent was a big boy, he would understand. Char realized at that moment that she desperately wanted to be the one to show Petra around, and get to know her better. She couldn't understand why she was so intrigued by her. Perhaps it was that she was a foreigner? Perhaps it was because she seemed too fascinating and beautiful, or that she was the type of rider that Char only dreamed of becoming. Char didn't know why, she just knew she was really drawn to her and wanted to spend as much time as possible with her.

Petra thought for a moment and then responded.

"Yes, thank you. That would be fabulous."

Char was equally delighted and terror-stricken simultaneously. She loved the thought of spending the afternoon with Petra but lamented the idea of having to disappoint her husband. She thought for two seconds and realized it would be worth it. She would simply send her husband a text and let him know that she had been held up at the barn. It could be for a myriad of reasons. She could make something up. Bottom line: nothing was going to stop her from spending the afternoon with Petra.

Chapter 12

Petra finished her last ride for the day around noon but still needed to put Erde away and get herself cleaned up. Char busied herself around the barn while waiting for Petra. There were always things to do, so filling her time while waiting was definitely not an issue. Seeing as it was a weekend, there were other riders taking lessons, and so Char had an opportunity to watch their lessons as well as learn by watching Petra teach. Later she spent some time cleaning her tack, organizing her locker area, and sweeping out the barn. At last, Petra closed the door after returning Erde to her stall and turned to Char.

"Ready?" she said, with her usual upbeat smile.

"Yes, absolutely!" Char responded. "Where do you want to go?"

Petra shrugged. "Mmmm, you be the leader, I don't know anything around here."

Char thought for a moment before responding.

"Ok then, how about lunch? Are you hungry?" Char could tell by Petra's positive expression that lunch was a great idea. "There's a place not too far from here, *La Boulangerie,* that has good croissant sandwiches, soups, and salads. How does that sound?"

"Yees!" Petra cheered. Even though Petra knew how to speak the language, every once in a while when she wasn't concentrating her accent would take over and simple words would be pronounced with a new twist. Char could listen to her talk for days! She absolutely loved her accent.

"All right," Char replied, matching her enthusiasm. "I'll drive."

The two women headed up towards the gate where the cars were parked and hopped in the car. Char was glad that the rain had abated for a while, and even though it was gray and foggy out, at least she didn't have to contend with the rain on top of the cold. Petra hopped into the passenger's side of the car after getting the gate for Char. With the gate safely latched behind them, they turned onto Dixon Lane and headed towards the coffee shop.

"So do you have French food in Germany?" Char asked, pointing to the sign, *La Boulangerie.*

"Yes of course," Petra responded, smirking. "We have pastries and baked goods, croissants, and such."

Char instantly felt her face flush for asking such an unworldly question. Embarrassed, she turned her attention to the large menu that was plastered to the wall behind the counter. Char ordered a large bowl of soup as she hoped it would warm her up. Petra ordered a turkey and cheese sandwich on a croissant. They found a small round table for two by a nearby window and sat down next to it, hoping to see outside. The rain had just begun and was steaming up the glass, causing little driblets to trickle into small miniature highways that ran vertically to the ground.

Even though she was a newcomer to the country and to California in par-ticular, Petra came across as adventurous and ready for new possibilities, as opposed to being timid. She wore a positive expression on her face virtually all the time. She was eager to speak even though her English was far from perfect, and she didn't seem bashful when it came to grammatical or articulation errors. Char, thinking about her own self-consciousness which caused her anxiety, wished she could learn to be more carefree.

As they began eating their lunch, Petra repeated the name of the restaurant to herself. "La Boulangerie," she said as if trying to add it to her memory so that she'd have at least one place she could venture to outside of the barn.

"So tell me about yourself, Char," she said.

Char paused, not sure where to start.

"Um, what do you want to know?" she asked.

"I don't know. Tell me something about you. Anything!"

Char thought for a moment and then replied.

"Well, first of all, I want you to know that I am really excited to have met you. I have always wanted to learn to ride dressage really well. Up until now, we have never had any trainers that knew dressage well or were upper-level riders, you know? We have had a few clinics from time to time, but mostly I have taken English lessons, and I really want to learn to ride like you. I am so excited you are here!"

Petra responded with a laugh, "Okay...but maybe you won't like me? Hmm? You don't even really know how I teach yet. I can be pretty tough and demand-ing with my students."

Char laughed back, not sure what to say. She already knew she liked Petra, a whole lot, in fact. Much more than she dared to confess to anyone, including herself. Char chalked it up to being fascinated with this woman from Europe, who brought so much mystique and intrigue to her world. Besides that, she was exactly the type of equestrian that Char hoped to be one day. If only her mother had allowed her when she was younger, and she hadn't gotten such a late start...who knows how far she could have taken it...

But Char didn't allow herself to drift too far back, lamenting what was already done. She had an opportunity now, and she was sitting right in front of her, eating a turkey croissant sandwich.

When lunch was over, Petra asked what time it was. Char looked at her watch and realized it was close to 3 o'clock. She jumped up, startled. *How could it possibly be so late already? Where had the day gone?*

Char couldn't believe it. It wasn't uncommon for time to fly by when she was at the stable and with her horse, but even this was extreme. Granted, she had told Kent where she was going, but by the time she brought Petra back and then drove home, it would be close to 4 p.m. Most of Saturday was gone, and she wondered what Kent would say. He had always been supportive of her time at the barn, but even she realized that this was pushing it a little too far. She would have to make it up to him tonight, she thought to herself. Ugh. The thought didn't excite her, but she owed it to him, she thought. It was the least she could do.

"Char? Did you hear me?" Petra asked. Char had been lost in her thoughts and had momentarily forgotten herself.

"Oh, yes. Ready?" She tried to pretend nothing was the matter. "Let's go then!"

The two drove the short distance back to Blue Ribbon and Char dropped Petra off at the gate, where it would be a quick walk up to her room off the Harrisons' main house.

"Well, okay then," Petra said, smiling. "See you whenever, I guess."

"Actually, I'll be out in the morning," Char said.

"Oh, okay then, I'll see you in the morning!"

Char backed out of the driveway and watched as Petra walked up to the door that led to her sleeping quarters, a private entrance off of the main house. She wondered what her room was like. Had she brought much with her? Had she decorated? Was it filled with horse photographs or pictures of her parents and sister back home? Char also wondered if Petra got lonely when she had no one else around. She made a mental note to talk to Kent about having her over for dinner. Char was eager for Petra to meet Kent and thought that having Petra over to the house would be a good idea. She made a point to ask Kent when she got home that afternoon and would have if things had gone the way she expected.

<h1 style="text-align:center">Chapter 13</h1>

Kent was angry. She could tell because he stayed at the far end of the house in the guest room watching TV, even when she called out to him.

"Kent? Hello!" she called into the back room. "Hey, it's me! I'm home." There was no answer, even though Char could hear the TV all the way in the kitchen.

Perhaps he fell asleep, Char said to herself, trying to convince herself even though she knew it wasn't true. He was a light sleeper to begin with, and also, he never took naps.

"Hey," she said gently when she finally made her way to the guestroom. She walked over to the side of the bed and kissed him gently. "How are you?" There was no answer, so she tried again. "Kent? You okay? What's going on?"

Kent still didn't respond, but took the remote and clicked it, turning off the television. Something must have really been on his mind for him to turn off a football game.

"You're never home," he said finally.

"Yes, I am. That's not true. I know I'm a little late today, but I tried calling earlier, and well, Petra hadn't been off the property and so I brought her to lunch. I'm sorry."

Still no response.

"Kent? I said I was sorry. What's wrong?"

There was an even longer silence, and then he said it. Kent actually brought to the forefront, the very topic that Char had been wanting to avoid. Sex.

"It's like you're not even...interested," he finally managed. "You never initiate anything, and it just feels like you are, I don't know, going through the motions, I guess."

Char was taken aback. She had not seen this coming. Especially not today. Things had been going so well, or so she thought. Yes, she had been preoccupied lately and busier than usual. But that was to be expected. After all, it isn't every day that a new transplant arrives from another country, one that you've been waiting your whole life for, to open up an entirely new world for you. Was he really that insecure? Or, jealous, perhaps?

Char didn't know what to say.

"Look," she finally managed after a long silence. "I know there has been a lot going on lately, and I know I've been preoccupied and busy, especially with everything going on at Blue Ribbon. But I promise you, it has nothing to do with how I feel about you. I mean it."

Kent slowly turned his head and made eye contact with Char.

"Really?" he said. "Are you sure about that?"

"Yes! Positive!" Just as the words were coming out, Char thought about them and felt disingenuous, the way you feel when you force a smile in hopes that your mood will follow. Perhaps her enthusiasm was designed to help her feel the words as if they were true. She quickly dismissed the thought and continued. "In fact, I was wondering how you would feel about us having Petra over for dinner, maybe next weekend? I'd really like for you to get to know her," she suggested.

Kent hesitated for a moment before answering. "Yeah, sure," he said. "If you want to. I guess that would be fine."

Char didn't want to start another argument when she had barely succeeded in ending this one, but she turned her back so she could roll her eyes. *Don't sound too enthusiastic,* she thought sarcastically to herself. Instead, she held her tone, and responded, "Great. I'll let her know. It should be fun."

Suddenly she was no longer in the mood to give Kent any pity sex tonight. Not with his indifferent attitude and hurt feelings all of a sudden. And for what? When she stopped to think about it, what had she really done that was so bad? Wasn't she entitled to have a little fun of her own once in a while? After all, she went to all of her husband's work engagements, took care of things around the house, and provided him with sex anytime he wanted it...although she was really beginning to reconsider the "anytime he wanted it" part of the deal. It wasn't like he ever went to any of her horse events, so no, she was not going to feel guilty.

The rest of the evening at home was uneventful, with both Char and Kent heading to bed early. Char did her best to busy herself with the kitchen and some last-minute clean-up before she went to bed, hoping that Kent would be asleep before she came into the room. Fortunately, she'd timed her entrance perfectly, and she detected the subtle difference in his breathing that alerted her that he was asleep, as she slipped silently beneath the covers next to him.

Chapter 14

"Teacher's pet!" was the first thing Char heard when she entered the barn on Monday morning.

"What are you talking about, Kim?" Char wasn't amused.

"Oh, sure, play innocent with me," Kim continued. "But the word is going around the barn that you took Petra out to lunch on Saturday. I see how it is! You two become pals and all of a sudden you'll be the favorite, getting all of the extra help and attention from the teacher..." she mocked in a tone that reminded Char of high school.

"Are you kidding me?" Char asked. Char wasn't sure if Kim was serious or joking. She'd better be joking, Char thought, or she was going to be angry. "Yeah, okay, it's about time that someone took the poor woman off the property! Did you know she literally hadn't been anywhere outside Blue Ribbon since she got here last week?" Char snapped back. *What was wrong with everyone lately?* she wondered. *Seriously!* They were all starting to piss her off.

"Hold your horses, my dear," Kim jeered. "Someone's wound a little tight this morning. You all right?"

"Yeah, I'm sorry, Kim," Char said, settling back down again. "It's just...I don't know. Something just isn't right between Kent and me. I mean, nothing is wrong, exactly, except that..."

"Except what?" Kim answered. By now, Char had gotten her attention, and Kim had stopped grooming her horse; all focus was now on Char.

"Well, I don't know." Char hesitated. "It's just that, well, he got mad at me yesterday. He thinks I'm spending too much time out here."

"Is that it?" Kim asked, incredulous.

"Well, no," Char admitted. "It's also the sex."

"What about it?"

"About how there isn't any. Or rather, how I wish there wasn't any…"

"Oh, Char!" Kim now sounded deeply concerned and saddened for her friend. "How long have you been feeling this way?"

"For a while now, I'll admit. But I thought it was quite common, you know, as couples age and have been together for a while. I thought things were supposed to…simmer down."

Kim shot Char a look of complete confusion. She had no idea what Char was talking about, as she and Jim were as sexual as ever. If anything, their intimacy had evolved to deeper levels over the years.

"Wow, Char," Kim finally responded, choosing her words carefully. "I don't know what to say. Have you ever considered marriage counseling?"

Char looked up just in time to see Sue coming down to ready her horse for a ride. She didn't know how much Sue had heard, but clearly enough.

"Who needs marriage counseling?" she shouted from the end of the barn. "Certainly not you, Kim. I've seen you and Jim on more than one occasion!"

Char wanted to die. Although she loved Sue, Sue was of a different generation, and she just wasn't ready to talk to Sue about her love life. Now everyone would know, and it could possibly get back to Joe, Petra, and whoever else happened to be around.

Char began to appeal to Sue. "Sue, please, don't say anything. It's nothing, really. Kent and I are just, well, I don't know exactly. We are just going through some…some things right now. It isn't anything that can't be worked out."

"I understand, my dear." Sue gave Char a knowing wink. "All marriages go through their tough spots, doll. You just hang in there. And you know that both Joe and I are always here for you if you should ever need to talk."

"I know." Char smiled at Sue. She felt genuinely lucky to have such a nice group of people to spend her days with. But that didn't mean she wanted to discuss it anymore, so she changed the subject by pretending she was behind schedule. "Oh wow," she said, throwing the saddle over Mystic. "I better hurry up. Gonna be late…"

And with that, Char and Mystic walked out of the barn.

Chapter 15

"**M**orning, Char!" Petra called cheerily from atop a rather large horse named Zeus.

"Good morning," Char returned the greeting, genuinely happy to see Petra. "Who is this?" she asked, nodding at Zeus. "This is Zeus," Petra said. "He is one of the warmbloods that I brought over with me from Germany. He is still only training-level dressage, but with his great size and build, he has a lot of potential. He is just four years old. Want to ride him?" Petra asked.

Char froze in her tracks, unable to respond. Of course, she wanted to ride him! A horse of this caliber, imported from Germany? Absolutely! He must have been worth at least 15 or 20 thousand, even without all of his training yet. Char could tell by the look of him that he was clearly a warmblood, and must have had papers that tracked his bloodline.

On the other hand, as much as she wanted to ride him, she was a bit intimidated. Surely Zeus would expose her flaws in her riding, maybe even take off with her, or equally embarrassing, not respond to her cues and refuse to move at all. Eventually, excitement overcame her anxiety, and Char looked again at Petra for confirmation, double-checking that she'd heard her right. By now Petra had dismounted and was holding the reins out toward Char.

"Are you sure?" was all Char could manage, walking slowly toward Zeus. She attempted to reach up to pet his nose, but he jerked his head upward so Char couldn't even reach his face for a quick pat on the nose as he was so tall.

"He is a bit head shy," Petra volunteered, slowly lowering Zeus's head and rubbing his face vigorously. Then, half talking to Zeus, she continued, "which is all the reason we need to love on you and rub your face, right big guy?" She turned to Char. "If a horse is afraid of something or has anxiety about it, we do not accept that. All the more reason we need to re-expose him to it over and over."

Char thought for a second and realized she had more in common with the horses than she thought. "Yes, I do know a thing or two about anxiety," she admitted. "I guess exposure therapy works the same way for the horses as it does for humans," she said.

By now Zeus had relaxed and his eyes were closing, his head now lowered to about two feet from the ground.

"You're sure about this?" Char questioned one final time.

"Absolutely!" Petra responded, confidently.

That was one thing that Char noticed about Petra: no matter what, she always was so confident. *How did she know?* Char thought to herself.

Then, as if reading her mind, Petra answered Char's question.

"Don't forget, I am a trainer. I will train you, and I will train the horse. If you want to learn properly, it is better for you to ride as many horses as you can."

"Okay," Char said, taking a deep breath and looking around for the mounting block.

"Never mind the mounting block," Petra said. "Here, step into my hand and I will help you," she said, lacing her hands together next to the side of Zeus for Char to step into.

Char hesitated.

"Come on, don't be shy," Petra encouraged. "Go ahead."

Char stepped into Petra's hands, which were laced together for Char to step into. She was used to getting up on horses this way when a mounting block wasn't available but felt somehow self-conscious putting the underside of her dirty shoe into Petra's hand. Char gave it a gallant effort and leaned in as she reached up for a handful of mane and rein, but Zeus's withers were so high she couldn't quite reach and therefore still needed a boost so that she would be high enough to swing her back leg over the saddle.

Petra instinctively released one of her hands once Char's foot was securely in the stirrup, and used it to push her butt up and towards the tall horse. After much struggle, Char's upper body leaned forward onto Zeus's neck, and from this position, she was finally able to swing her leg up and over the other side.

"Whew! That was difficult. I should have just used the mounting block," Char said, thinking about Petra's hand on her butt, and feeling slightly embarrassed.

"Don't worry!" Petra shared. "Remember, I do this for a living. Well, not pushing people in the butt, but it does come with the territory," she laughed.

Char gave Zeus a gentle squeeze with her leg, encouraging a forward motion. Without hesitation Zeus began a forward walk, pushing forward and not pulling. The feeling of sitting atop a horse who was using his body correctly was something Char seldom felt in riding her own horse, and the feeling was absolutely amazing, even at a simple walk. Zeus was very responsive to her cues, and his head and neck felt very light in her hands. She never wanted this feeling to end. Petra was unusually quiet and after a few minutes, Char was ready for some feedback.

"So, do you have any suggestions?" she asked.

Instead of answering, Petra asked her a question in return.

"What do you think? Hmm?"

"Um, well, this feels amazing!" Char said, her eyes still focused on the arena that lay before her.

"Then that should answer your question," was Petra's only response.

In the meantime, Petra hopped onto Mystic and started warming him up, asking for more bend, stretching, and engagement than he usually offered. It was incredible to see the potential in her horse and the transformation right before her eyes, after just a few moments with Petra on his back. If only she could learn how to make her horse move this way...

The hour flew by and before Char knew it, it was time for Petra's next lesson. The two traded their horses back and Char was still floating from the wonderful ride when she finally remembered that she was supposed to invite Petra over for dinner.

"Oh, hey," Char said, almost as an afterthought. "My husband, Kent and I would like to have you over for dinner sometime. Would you be interested?"

"Let me think," Petra teased. "I just came to the United States from Germany and I know no one other than you, and Sue and Joe, and a couple of the boarders. I haven't left the property except for the one time that you and I went to La Boulangerie for lunch. So yeah, I would be delighted."

Char smiled. "Okay, then. Tomorrow night?"

"Tomorrow night it is." Petra smiled in agreement.

Char left the barn later that day but couldn't take her mind off of the morning that she'd had. Petra was turning out to be everything Char had hoped for as a rider, person, and trainer. The feeling of riding atop Zeus was one she would relish endlessly until the next time, which she hoped would be as soon as possible.

Chapter 16

It was a rare day that Char didn't go out to the barn, at least for a little bit. Even if she didn't ride, she'd still usually stop by to turn Mystic out to run around and get out of his stall for a while. Although he had a paddock attached to his stall which allowed for a little outdoor time, it wasn't nearly sufficient for him to do much other than see what was going on around him. But today Char was busy getting ready to have Petra over for dinner to meet Kent, and she wanted everything to be just perfect. Mystic would have to wait until tomorrow.

It was nearly 5 o'clock and Char knew that Petra would be arriving any moment when Char's cell phone rang. Char hoped it wasn't Petra, canceling their dinner. Surprisingly, when she looked at her phone, she saw that it was Kent.

"Hey, Char, I'm really sorry," Kent said apologetically, but I'm going to have to stay late at the hospital tonight. I have a complicated surgery in the morning, and I am just not ready. I need to meet with a few of the other surgeons and come up with a game plan. Unfortunately, I'm going to have to spend a few more hours at the hospital."

Char stood there for a moment, not knowing what to say. She was so disappointed, but at the same time knew how hard her husband worked, and that if it weren't for him, she wouldn't have a horse trainer (or horse for that matter) in the first place.

After taking a moment to rethink and process the evening, she finally responded.

"Okay," she said, with a downcast tone to her voice. "I was really excited for you to meet Petra, but I understand."

"I know you do, honey. And don't worry, I'll make it up to you. I'll come out to the barn with you sometime, on the weekend, if I have to. I can meet Paula, I mean, Petra, then."

At that precise moment, the doorbell rang. Kent could hear it on the other end of the phone. "I'll let you go," he said. "See you later tonight."

"See you later," Char replied softly while walking over to answer the door.

As always, a cheerful Petra stood on the other side, looking absolutely stunning. Other than the one night at the party at the Harrisons' house, Char had only seen Petra in her riding clothes. Tonight she was freshly showered and smelled of...*was it lavender?* she wondered. Petra's face was freshly washed and devoid of the usual dirt and sweat, revealing a beautiful golden glow on her tanned skin. Her hair was extra bouncy after having just been washed, and she looked comfortable in her loose-fitting sweater and khakis. Petra stood there smiling, holding a bottle of wine in one hand and a small, store-bought plant in the other. It looked like a lily of some sort, but Char wasn't sure. Char was still processing what had just happened with her husband's quick announcement only to find Petra standing outside her living room.

"Are you going to let me in?" Petra asked, after standing at the door longer than was comfortable without an invitation.

"Oh, yes," Char fumbled. "Please, let me take that for you," she said, reaching for the wine and the plant. "You are too kind!"

Petra didn't respond but looked around the living room and kitchen before commenting, "Nice house. So where is your husband?"

"Thank you," Char said, as she opened the bottle of wine and set the plant on the counter. "Unfortunately, he just called to say that he's stuck at work. I'm afraid you'll have to meet him another time."

"Oh no!" Petra said, looking genuinely upset that she wouldn't be meeting Kent. "Perhaps we should reschedule? I can always come back another time."

"No, don't be silly!" Char said. "You can meet him another time. In fact, he said he might come out to the barn this weekend to make up for tonight. You can meet him then."

"All right," Petra said, accepting the glass of wine that was handed to her. "But I didn't want you to go to all this trouble for just me."

"Honestly," Char said, "it isn't any trouble at all. Look, I already made a chicken salad, pasta, and French bread. It's all done, so we can just relax and get to know each other better."

After noting how casual Petra looked, Char took stock of her own attire and decided that perhaps she was overdressed. She had on a collared white blouse, a long vintage necklace, and some dress slacks. She excused herself for a moment and walked into her bedroom to throw on a sweatshirt.

"You're cold?" Petra asked.

"Well, not yet," Char confessed. "But I do get chilled easily, so I thought I'd grab this sweatshirt, just in case."

Char then sat down on the couch next to Petra, still feeling nervous. Being with Petra was so exciting, seeing as she was international and this accomplished horse rider and all. She didn't know what to say, so she looked nervously around the room, avoiding eye contact.

"What about you?" she asked suddenly. "Are you cold?"

"No," Petra responded.

"Good."

Char finished her glass of wine and got up to get another. She brought the bottle over and noticed that Petra was not far behind her. She poured them both another round. Char could feel the wine as it hit her stomach, which had been empty for most of the day. This meant that not only could she feel the wine going to her stomach, but she could feel it rising to her head too. She felt herself begin to relax. She was just thinking about getting the pasta out of the oven when Petra spoke.

"So your husband, did I hear that he is a doctor?"

"Yes. A surgeon, actually. He's been practicing for the past five years now."

"I am disappointed he is not here tonight. I was hoping to talk to him about the arm that I broke a few years back. It is healed, but it still bothers me from time to time."

"I don't know, exactly," Char admitted, "but I'm sure he would be happy to help you in any way he can."

"That would be fabulous," Petra said, gazing directly into Char's eyes.

Char got up and went into the kitchen to break the uncomfortableness she felt with Petra's eyes on her. She wondered if that was a cultural nuance she wasn't familiar with. She'd have to Google it later after Petra had gone home. Perhaps it was part of the German culture, she considered, to be very direct that way. Regardless, she'd have to get used to it. She simply couldn't go running out of the room to break eye contact every time Petra made her nervous.

Five minutes later, Char returned with the last of the bottle of wine and refilled each of their glasses, announcing that dinner was ready. Char and Petra moved to the dining room table and sat down. Char lit a candle in the center as she always did when having a nice meal or company over, and they began to eat.

"Yum!" Petra was looking at Char, nodding up and down in agreement while chewing on a large bite of pasta. "This is delicious! It makes me miss being home already!"

"You had a lot of pasta in Germany?" Char asked inquisitively.

"Well, no. But we had spaetzle and schnitzel. Your home cooking reminds me of home. That's all. But it's very good!"

There was something about Petra that made Char just fascinated by her. She couldn't get over it, but the more time she spent with her, even outside the arena, the more time she continued to want to spend with her. She was beginning to feel like some sort of foreign horse groupie. She figured as Petra became more immersed in America and American culture she would branch out, and Char might not have this opportunity to hang out with her. She was happy to have this opportunity now, to soak everything in.

Kent was still not home from work by the time dinner had ended, and it was getting late, so Petra decided it was time to go.

"Hold on," Char said. "I will walk you to your car. It is dark outside and Kent usually does it, but since he's not here I'll walk out with you."

Char and Petra walked out to Petra's little car, something she had picked up inexpensively after arriving in the States.

"That's not going to haul many horses around," Char joked.

"Yeah, I know," Petra agreed. "I'll have to get something bigger as soon as I save up some money. Thank you for a wonderful evening, Char," Petra said, with her blue eyes fixed on Char's, even in the dark.

Petra leaned in to hug Char goodbye. And when she did, she planted a kiss squarely on Char's mouth. Char couldn't help but notice how soft her lips were, and she could feel her breath, which smelled sweet. Without saying another word, Petra then got in her car and drove away. And just like that, she was gone.

Chapter 17

Char turned around in the dark and walked back to her front door and into the house. She touched her hand to her lips and held it there for a moment, as her mind froze on the memory of the kiss that had occurred only moments before. She was stunned, and uncertain whether that kiss on the lips was a part of European custom, or if she had just been kissed romantically by Petra. She would try to shrug it off, walk a few steps, and then stop again.

"Nah," she kept saying to herself. *No way,* she thought. *That has to be part of the culture.* She would then try to move on, not make any more out of it than it was when suddenly she would stop again, frozen. Only her mind was racing. She kept telling herself it was nothing, but then there was that little voice in her head that told her otherwise. On a visceral level, she knew it was more. She couldn't explain it, she just had a vibe. Perhaps it was the way that Petra had looked at her across the room at dinner, or the fact that she maintained eye contact for a bit too long to be comfortable. Whatever it was, she knew that there had been several of these moments during the evening in which she tried to downplay a feeling she had as simply a cultural misunderstanding.

Char turned off the kitchen faucet, dried her hands, and walked over to her computer. She opened up a search engine, Google, and typed in the following words: *German customary greetings.* This would give her the answers that she knew in her head to be true, even when her gut was telling her something else.

Her first search turned up a quick list of common greetings. *There!* she said to herself, pointing at the computer. "Greeting #10: Some Germans, particularly younger Germans, use the Italian greeting, 'Ciao,' borrowed from the Italians."

That's it! she thought to herself. *I bet she has also adopted some of their other greetings too!* She remembered that Italians always kiss each other, on not one but *both* cheeks. She relaxed with this thought for just a moment until it dawned on her that this was *not* at all what was going on. Petra had kissed her squarely on the mouth. If she had been trying to emulate the Italians and missed her cheek in the dark, surely she would have then attempted to give her another kiss on the other cheek, right?

But she didn't. There was only one kiss. And it had been carefully placed squarely on her mouth without apology.

Char didn't know what to think of this, but suddenly she felt extremely tired and decided she no longer wanted to mull it over anymore. She returned to the kitchen to finish the dishes. She then headed straight to bed. Placing her head on the soft satin pillow was the last thing she knew until she woke the next morning.

Chapter 18

Char woke up the next morning as usual. She had forgotten about the strange end to her evening last night when Kent asked, "So how was your date with Petra?"

Char was taking a sip of coffee and nearly choked on Kent's words. Suddenly feeling defensive, she replied, "It wasn't a date!"

"You know what I mean," he said playfully. "Tell me how it went."

"Oh, it went fine," Char said as she walked toward her husband. "I missed you though," she added, trying to make things appear as normal as possible. Any perceived awkwardness and she would have some explaining to do. She certainly did not want to be put in that position this morning, particularly when she could be overreacting to the entire ordeal.

"All right," Kent was preoccupied, already thinking about his workday ahead. "I'm glad you had a nice time," he said. He slugged down the remainder of his black coffee that was still hot, kissed Char on the forehead, and headed out the door.

Not that I'm complaining, Char thought sarcastically to herself, *but I'm getting more intimacy from the horse trainer than I am my husband right now.*

Char really didn't mind. She knew Kent had plenty to think about with his surgery today and was focused on that. Besides, she didn't want to have to immerse herself in conversation this morning anyway. She was too caught up in her own head trying to make sense of what had happened last night by the car.

As she readied herself to head out to the stable, she kept thinking about it and then trying not to think about it. Thinking about it didn't help, and not thinking about it was, well, impossible. She decided she would head out to the barn as usual and act the same way she always did. Friendly, but not too friendly. The last thing she wanted to do was create any awkwardness.

Char was happy to see Kim's car already parked when she pulled up around 10 a.m., later than usual, at Blue Ribbon. But instead of being in the barn or riding in the arena, Kim was sitting on the patio with Sue, overlooking Petra, who was down below in the arena doing a warmup routine with one of her horses that Char didn't recognize. When Char got out of her car, Kim and Sue waved, and Char decided to go over and join the two in conversation.

As Char approached, she pulled out a chair, and could easily tell by the two women's expressions that things were not the status quo.

"What's going on?" Char asked, concerned.

"It's Jim," Kim replied, serious and looking worried. Her mouth was tight and little beads of sweat were forming on her upper lip. Her brow was furrowed, and she kept gazing downward at the table.

Instantly, Char panicked. "Is he okay?" she asked, thinking he might have had a heart attack or some other physical malady.

"No," she said. "It's not that...it's the business. It's being audited, and there have already been several findings."

Char didn't know much about business or finance, but she knew the words "audit" and "finding", and knew that they weren't good. She sat quietly, waiting for Kim to continue.

"I don't know what to do," she said, panic-stricken. "We could lose everything if they shut us down. The business, our house, DiMaggio..."

As sweet and as motherly as ever, Sue instantly tried to relieve some of the financial pressure from her friend.

"Now Kimberly," she said. "Don't you worry about your boarding fees this month. You just sit tight until you get things figured out. It will work out, you'll see," she said, patting Kim's hand.

Kim was staring down at her feet. Sue and Char managed to share a worried look across the table without Kim noticing. Sue's look defied her words, which had been so soothing and comforting. But from across the table, Char could tell that Sue was very concerned for Kim.

"I'm sorry," was all Char could think of after sitting quietly for several minutes. This startling news was the first thing that had distracted her from the kiss last night that she couldn't get out of her mind. When Char finally looked up and saw Petra down in the arena, expertly performing a pirouette on her horse, Char had an instant burst of butterflies flutter in her stomach. She shook noticeably and quickly looked away before Petra looked up and saw herself being watched. She didn't want Petra to notice that she had caught Char's attention.

Kim stood up to go, and so Sue went back to the house and Char said goodbye.

"Hang in there, friend," she said. "Call me later, okay?"

Kim said she would. Char wasn't so sure, so she vowed to call her later that day to see how Kim was holding up.

Char now was faced with walking down along the side of the arena, where she debated saying hello to Petra. She didn't want to be rude, but she didn't want to interrupt her riding either.

"Hey," she finally said, as casually as she could manage, when their eyes accidentally met as Petra rounded the corner near where Char was walking on the other side of the railing.

"Hello!" Petra called back, cheerful as normal.

Char continued to walk into the barn but now her head was racing again.

Maybe she really thinks nothing of it! she thought. *Perhaps it really is just me, and I am making far too big a thing out of this.*

At that moment she decided to put "the kiss" behind her once and for all. She focused her attention on the task at hand, which was readying Mystic for her lesson today. She even allowed herself to focus on Kim, momentarily. Char couldn't believe it. Kim and Jim had always seemed like the perfect couple. There was just no way this could be happening. Char certainly hoped it was all a big misunderstanding. The auditors would find something that would clear the company's name, and everything would go back to being as it should be. Kim and Jim were decent people, for Pete's sake. Better than decent, even. They were good people. Char knew in her heart they had not done anything wrong, at least not intentionally.

There was a lower part of the property that flooded every year, but as it was nearing February by now without so much as a drop of rain in the past month, Char ventured down the path to the meadow that lay below the barn, down and around a bend that was out of sight and more woodsy than the rest of the property. It was still early in the morning and the grass smelled sweet. Little droplets of dew wet her boots as she walked through with Mystic. The sun was shining, but not enough to warm the air sufficiently. She could still see her breath as she exhaled, and she didn't dare remove her jacket. She checked her watch. She still had at least 20 minutes before her lesson. It would be just enough time to let Mystic run around in the pasture and play before walking him back up to the arena for their training.

Down here in the meadow, far from the barn and activity of the house, Char looked around and took it all in. It was so quiet and peaceful, with only the sounds of the birds and the vision of sunlight sparkling off the overgrown grass to enjoy. Mystic was equally at peace. He stopped once as he had heard a noise.

He then raised both his head and tail up, stiffened, and took off in a gallop into the trees beyond. Char was standing still holding his halter in her left hand and his reins in her right when she suddenly felt a presence behind her.

She reacted by turning and looking over her right shoulder to find Petra standing just beyond, seemingly enjoying the moment too. Startled to now find that she wasn't alone, Char stiffened and checked her watch once more.

"Oh, I'm sorry," she said. "Is it time for my lesson already? I had just checked my watch a moment ago and..."

Before Char could finish, Petra interrupted her.

"No, not at all," she said. "I just wanted to see you, alone."

Char gulped quietly, trying not to choke on her own saliva. She was nervous. She didn't know exactly what Petra was going to say, although she now had a strong suspicion. She could not bring herself to say anything out loud. Her heart was beating quickly and she suddenly felt her adrenaline pumping inside her. It was hard to stand still. Quiet. She shivered. So instead, she pretended not to know. She glanced at Petra briefly, and then, pretending to be focused on Mystic, said, "Oh. Is everything okay? If you have to cancel the lesson, I understand."

Petra walked slowly toward Char, smiling. When she reached Char, she glanced down at the reins in her hand and reached out to take them from her.

"Allow me," she said gently, taking the reins from her. Petra, holding the reins now, turned in the direction of Mystic and watched too. The two stood silent for several moments before Petra spoke again.

Just standing there quietly next to Petra, Char felt a strange energy, an exchange of some sort, connecting them. It was difficult to sort out. It was pleasant, and she didn't want to move away, but she didn't know what it was, what to call it. It was a new feeling. So instead of moving away, she stood there, nervous, trembling almost, until Petra reached over and put her arm around Char's shoulders.

"Cold?" she asked.

"Um, not exactly," Char responded, not able to turn towards Petra. So she stood there frozen, trying not to move. She kept her eyes focused on Mystic, who was now grazing contentedly off in the distance.

"You're shivering," Petra noted, turning towards Char.

"Am I?" Char was caught. She couldn't run, she couldn't hide, she couldn't deny what was happening.

"I am just going to get this out in the open," Petra finally said. "Are you...you know..." she hesitated.

"Am I what?" Char now turned to face Petra directly.

"Mmmm, I don't know the word, in English," Petra said, searching. "You know, it's like when a boy loves a boy, that sort of thing."

"What, gay? No! Petra!" Char couldn't believe this was happening. By now Char's heart was really racing and she was completely amped up on adrenaline. "No! Absolutely not! Why would you even ask me that?" Char was emphatic. She was practically yelling by now. But before she could protest anymore, she felt those same lips from last night, those same soft and warm lips, with the intoxicating breath behind them, entering into her nose, her mouth, her everything. Suddenly she couldn't think straight, because her senses and desires had taken over. She had now lost control, and was outside herself, observing herself not just receiving Petra's kiss, but returning it herself, with her arms feeling her body, her back, her shoulders. Suddenly she was dizzy. She forced herself away from the pull, which felt gravitational. It was so hard to pull...pull...pull, finally...away. She stopped and wiped her face with the back of her hand, staring Petra squarely in the face now. She had lost all focus on Mystic. She was facing Petra, searching her eyes, and her mind was alternately spinning too fast and not functioning at all. She was in complete shock. She was pretty sure that kiss wasn't German or Italian, but rather...French! What was going on?

After several minutes of standing still, frozen and shocked, Char found that she could move again. She slowly picked up the halter that she had dropped, and began walking, slowly, mechanically, towards Mystic.

"Char, wait," Petra followed her, reaching her shoulder.

Char kept walking, seemingly incoherent. "Uh, no, I can't. I have to go get Mystic. I have to go." She continued walking toward her horse. Char was so startled and so confused by her own emotions, by what had just happened. *Oh my god, Kent!* she thought. Her mind was so preoccupied that she didn't see the hole in the ground that lay just in front of her, and she stepped into it, twisting her ankle. The next thing she knew, she was writhing on the ground in pain, screaming in agony. She tried to get up and walk, but she couldn't.

Chapter 19

The next thing Char knew, she was waking up in an unfamiliar setting. The room was small, with several windows and a door that led outside. There was a small twin bed in the corner that she had been placed on, with a microwave on top of a desk, and a small refrigerator on the ground. She looked out the window and realized where she was. She was still at Blue Ribbon.

Char opened her eyes and lay in the little bed, still, trying to sort out what was fact and what was fiction. Had she dreamed the kiss in the meadow, down by the lower pasture? Did she fall off her horse and hit her head? How did she get here? She didn't even remember. She lay in the bed, trying to sort it all out when Petra noticed she was awake.

"How are you feeling?" Petra said, leaning in next to Char.

"Confused," Char replied. "What happened?"

"The truth?" Petra asked, "We were kissing in the meadow, down by the pasture. Actually, I kissed you, and then you were kissing me back when you suddenly pulled away. You then started walking, sort of in a daze, when you tripped and fell. You twisted your ankle, but when you fell, you fell back and knocked your head on this rock here. You must have passed out because Jose came and got you on the back of his flatbed, and drove you up here."

"Does anyone know?" Char asked.

"No, I don't kiss and tell," Petra replied. "I told Jose you fell off your horse. Look," she said, holding up the reins, "The reins must have slipped off when you were out riding, and you fell. It was unfortunate that you landed on this rock and hit your head."

Char didn't respond, but continued to lay there and felt her head. It was extremely tender with a golf ball-sized welt.

"Does Kent know?" she asked.

"Yes, of course," Petra said. "He's your husband. And a doctor, right? He's on his way. He should be here to get you soon."

Char sat up and began to panic. Everything was happening so fast and she didn't have time to think. Couldn't think.

Petra must have seen the panic on Char's face because she suddenly added, "Don't worry. I didn't tell him anything. I told him you fell off your horse."

Char didn't respond but continued to lay in the bed, wondering how in the world the day had turned out like this. Within minutes there was a knock at the door. Char could see through the window that it was Kent, here to take her home.

"Hello," Petra said warmly. "Kent? I'm sorry. I didn't imagine I would be meeting you under these conditions. It seems she had a little fall, but nothing out of the ordinary. I think she will be okay."

Kent nodded at Petra and smiled, not saying a word. His focus was already on Char, and he wanted to speak with her instead.

"Hi, honey," he said tenderly. "Are you all right? I came as soon as I could. Let's get you home and I'll check you out, make sure you're all right, okay? If we need to I can always bring you by the hospital, get a quick x-ray, all right?"

Char nodded. She felt too guilty, too tired, and too much in pain to try and argue with anyone. All she wanted to do right now was to go back to sleep and escape from this miserable day.

Kent brought her home and placed her in bed. He checked her over, and when he was convinced it was nothing serious other than some bumps and bruises, he kissed her goodbye and headed back to the hospital. Char, on the other hand, was thankful to be left alone for a bit to get her senses about her and do some soul searching in order to try and figure out what was going on and how she was feeling about, well, just about everything.

She tried to sleep but kept tossing and turning. Her head hurt and her ankle was swollen. Her emotions were raw and she wanted to cry. After lying in bed for several hours, she picked up the phone and called her friend Valerie.

"Hello?" Valerie answered the phone, breathing heavily.

"Hey, Val," Char said, trying to sound cheerful. "I either caught you having sex with some hot new dude, or you are working out."

"Funny," Valerie said laughing. "I only wish I was having sex with some hot new dude. But you'd be the first to hear about it! What's up?"

"Do you have a minute?"

"Yeah, of course. Everything okay?"

"Not exactly," Char confessed. "I'm calling you because I'm hurt. I mean, I'm hurt, but that's not why I'm calling, exactly. Rather, I have a bit of a...I don't know...a situation, and I don't know what to do."

"I'm listening," Valerie said, her breath becoming more steady than when she'd first answered the phone.

"Okay, so I like totally don't know how to put this Valerie, so are you sitting down?"

"Alright. I'm sitting. Hurry up already, you're starting to scare me."

"Hold on, hold on, give me a second. This is tough. I honestly don't know what happened."

"Something with you and Kent?"

"You could say that, I guess, but not exactly."

"He didn't cheat on you, did he? Pick up on some floozy nurse at the hospital, did he?"

"No, no, no, it's not Kent. Kent's great."

"Then what? Who is it then?"

"Do you remember Petra? I mentioned her to you?"

"Petra, the new horse trainer from Germany? Yeah, I remember. What about her?"

"We...we...we..." Char tried to force herself to spit it out, but couldn't.

Growing impatient, Valerie interrupted, "You what? Spit it out, girl!"

"Okay, okay...hold on a sec...we...we kissed!"

The next thing Char knew she heard such uproarious laughter on the other end of the phone that she had to hold it away from her ear as far as she could. She waited for what felt like forever for the laughter to stop. Finally, she could hear Valerie winding down on the other end, so she pulled the phone closer to her ear again.

"Valerie! What's so funny? It's not funny! Why are you laughing!"

"Ahahahahahahah!" The laughter began again. Again, Char removed the phone from her ear to avoid it hurting from all the noise.

"Ha..ha...okay. Sorry, Char," Valerie said. "Hold on a sec, I have to wipe my eyes. I'm crying from laughing so hard. You are so funny! She's from Germany, silly! That's what they do there! It's their custom! It's Europe, honey! Hello!"

"So they French kiss everyone they meet?" Char interrupted. Suddenly the laughter came to an abrupt halt. There was silence on the other end.

"Wait, what?" Valerie asked, this time shocked. "Are you serious? She Frenched you? As in a French kiss? Are you sure?"

Now Char was the one laughing, and rolling her eyes at her friend. "What do you mean, am I sure? Valerie! I wasn't born yesterday! Yes, of course, I'm sure! Don't you think I'd know the difference between a friendly kiss and a French kiss?"

Valerie was suddenly deadly serious. "Oh my god. What did you tell Kent?"

"What do you mean? 'What did I tell Kent?' Nothing! I told Kent absolutely nothing! What do you think, I'm stupid? Of course, I didn't tell him!"

"Wow, Char," Valerie said, quietly. "I don't know what to say. Really, I'm surprised. I honestly didn't see this coming."

"Neither did I," Char confessed. "And Val?"

"Yeah?"

"I think I liked it, sort of. I'm not sure."

"Well, what happened after the kiss?"

"I don't know."

"What do you mean you don't know?"

"I mean, I don't know. I think I passed out."

The sound of laughter once again filled Char's ears at a higher decibel than before. Valerie couldn't control her laughter, and the sounds echoed in Char's ears for a long time. Char held the phone away from her head, trying to soften the sound. She waited for the laughter on the other end to stop. Instead, after several minutes, Char heard a "click," and then there was silence. Valerie had laughed so hard that she had accidentally hung up the phone. Char glanced at her own phone and hung it up too. She rolled over in bed and tried to fall back asleep.

Chapter 20

Kim was in the tack room pulling things out and putting them into a big box when Sue walked in.

"Kim?" she asked cautiously. "What's going on?"

"Oh, Sue!" Kim stood up and turned to face her. Her eyes were puffy and red. Tears were still streaming down her face, and the end of her nose was irritated and shiny too. Kim tried to speak, but the words wouldn't come out. She put her tissue up to wipe her nose and sobbed some more.

"Aw, Kim!" Sue said, reaching out to embrace her. "Slow down, slow down. What is all this?" she asked. "Come on, let's go sit down and talk." Sue motioned to a bench that was inside the tack room, commonly used for resting horse paraphernalia or to change clothing. She summoned Kim to sit down. "What in the world is the matter? What could possibly have you this upset? And you're cleaning out your tack room? Come on girl, we need to slow down and figure this out." Kim looked up at Sue between tears and tried to explain.

"There's no use," she cried. "It's all over, everything! My marriage, my horse, you...even the Mercedes!" She began crying pitifully again.

"My dear, my dear, hold on just a minute here. Slow down. This must be in reference to the audit you told me about, the one at Jim's work?"

"Yes," Kim cried, sobbing. "It's all over, everything!" Kim leaned forward and lay down on the bench, her body trembling with anguish. She was sobbing so hard now that Sue was worried she might not catch her breath, maybe even hyperventilate. Sue reached over and began trying to comfort Kim, rubbing her back, cooing to her softly.

"There, there...It'll be all right," she said. Sue looked up in despair as she was at a loss for words when she saw Petra walk in.

"What happened?" Petra asked. "Did she fall off her horse? Do we need an ambulance?"

Sue shook her head and whispered "No," and continued rubbing Kim on her backside. Kim was still crying loudly and hadn't moved from her forward position on the hard bench.

As Petra didn't know Kim all that well yet, she didn't want to intrude. After she could see that there was no physical injury, Petra backed out of the room, quietly, but whispered to Sue, "Let me know if you need anything."

Kim continued sobbing for another 15 minutes before Sue could hear that her breaths were calming, and the noises coming from her crying had settled a little. By now there was a huge wet puddle on the bench and on the ground from her tears. After another five minutes, Kim sat up and said simply, "It's over. Jim was embezzling money. Sue, I'm so scared, I don't know what I'm going to do."

<h1 style="text-align:center">Chapter 21</h1>

It was half-past seven when the phone rang and Char was still in bed, trying to decide if she was in more emotional or physical pain. The pain in her head and on her ankle was still a reminder of the day's events, which then brought her face to face with her emotional state, which was also in agony.

"Hello?" she said, without bothering to see who it was.

"Char? How are you?" Sue's voice on the other end sounded concerned.

"I'm okay," Char said. She hoped that news of "the kiss" hadn't yet made its way around the barn.

"You took quite a fall this morning I heard. Any permanent damage?"

"No, I don't think so. Kent took me home and checked me out. Other than a slight bump on my head and a sore ankle, I think I'm going to be all right. But you sound like something is bothering you, Sue. What's going on?" Char knew Sue well enough to tell when she was worried about something.

"Can you keep a secret, Char? It's Kim. I just have to tell someone. I can't keep this to myself."

"Well Sue," Char responded, "if it's about the audit at Kim and Jim's work, I already know there's some potentially bad stuff going on. Kim already shared that with us the other day."

"Yeah, that's true, Char. But there's more."

"What do you mean, more?"

"Are you sitting down?" Sue asked.

"Yeah. Well, lying down, actually, but go ahead." By now Char thought about sitting up, as she could tell this was big. She started to but the pounding in her head stopped her.

"Kim and Jim, they're done. Over. As in 'finito.'"

"Shut up!" Char replied, managing to bring herself to a sitting position with the use of a properly placed pillow. "They were the happiest couple I've ever seen! Kim's life was perfect! What in the world could have happened?"

"Kim found out that Jim has been embezzling client money."

"Holy crap!" Char let out a yell, forgetting momentarily about her head. It was now pounding due to her yelling.

"Yeah, she's a complete mess," Sue acknowledged. "I'm really, really, worried about her."

"Oh my god," Char said, lying back down again. The two minutes of sitting, combined with her inadvertent yelling, was about all her head could take at the moment.

"Okay, all right, I'll think of something," she said.

"Yeah, I know," Sue said. "Me too. I'll talk to you soon."

"Bye, Sue."

"Bye."

No sooner had Char put down the phone and began to ponder the day's events (*what a day!* She thought to herself), than could she hear the garage go up and Kent driving in.

"Hey," he said lovingly when he walked in, "and how is my at-home patient doing tonight?" he asked Char.

Between her pain and now Kim's situation, Char had momentarily forgotten about the drama (is that what it was?) between her and Petra. For the moment, she preferred to leave it that way, as it was one too many things for her to be able to focus on at the moment.

"I'm hanging in there," she said, "but I just got some really bad news. Kim and Jim are splitting up. Turns out that Jim has been embezzling money from his company. It sounds like they are losing everything: their house, their marriage, the horses, their dream, everything! Kim is a huge mess. I wouldn't be surprised if Jim is even looking at jail time."

Kent was in the midst of taking off his tie when he heard the news. He turned and faced Char, and looked so sad about what he'd just heard.

"Oh my goodness," he said. "Wow. I'm absolutely stunned. They'd seemed so perfect, you know? What is she going to do?"

"I don't know," was all Char could muster at the moment. Char had been asking herself the same question as it pertained to her feelings for Petra.

"Well, I'll tell you what," Kent announced decidedly. "She is your friend and the victim. She is welcome to stay with us until she gets back on her feet."

"Are you serious?" Char asked. *Why was her husband so adorable, so sweet, especially when it just made her situation harder?* Char didn't like that she was attracted, no, rather, *interested?* in Petra, especially when she had such a perfect husband. She knew it was unfair to him. At the same time, she'd been wondering for a while if she'd made a mistake. And now that Petra had arrived it had just stirred up something within her that had been missing, excitement and passion she had been longing for. Char wondered if she was confusing her passion and excitement for the horses and mistakenly placing these feelings on Petra. Was that possible? But clearly, Petra had feelings for her too. So perhaps it was something more? She just didn't know. And with everything that had gone on today, she was both physically and emotionally drained. Yes, she would let Kim know that she was more than welcome to move in with her and Kent for the time being. At least one thing was settled. With no more energy to try and solve any of the other issues that were swirling around in her mind, Char rolled over and closed her eyes again, this time not to awake until morning.

Chapter 22

It had been three days since Char had left the house. Three days since she'd gone out to see Mystic. Three days since she'd kissed Petra. And Char was as confused as ever. She wasn't ready to see Petra yet, as her mind was still spinning and she needed more time. More time to digest what she was feeling, more time to consider things. Not wanting to lead Petra, or Kent for that matter, one way or another, she was afraid of saying or doing the wrong thing either way, leading one of them on, or off, that she just wanted to stay far away from both until she knew.

But she couldn't. Mystic was waiting for her. She was absolutely never gone this long. She was out at Blue Ribbon practically every day, even if she wasn't riding. At the very least, she would come out to turn him out in the pasture, give him his grain, or check on him to see if the weather was too cold or too warm and his blanket needed to be taken off or put back on. This whole business of avoiding the stable for three days had to end. It was unacceptable to her, and to her treatment of her horse. Char decided it was time to get out of the house and take care of business, like it or not. Which was precisely the problem.

Did she like it? The kiss, the intoxication, the excitement, the newness of this foreigner? Of this woman? Or did she dislike what it was doing to her? Causing her to question, making her feel things she had never felt before? Making her doubt her own decisions and what she wanted? A possible threat to the life, the wonderful life, that she already had? She didn't know. So her plan was to keep her head down. Get in, and get out. Be friendly, but not overly, and certainly not rude. Inside she was all jitters, excited to see Petra again. She missed the intoxication that Petra gave her. On the other hand, she must keep these feelings hidden. It was forbidden love, and for that she was ashamed. She didn't want anyone to know. Especially not now, when she didn't know what she wanted herself. She needed time. Much more time to think. Unfortunately, she didn't have that luxury, as Mystic needed her, and she wasn't going to neglect this beautiful creature that was her responsibility.

When she pulled up at the gate and got out to open it, she couldn't stop herself. She glanced over, and there she was. Her heart began to race. She was excited and wanted to see her, to be near her, to spend time with her. She knew it was wrong, and so willed it away, but she couldn't. Her eyes followed her as long as the line of sight allowed. She was moving swiftly and gracefully atop Erde, practicing her half passes and canter pirouettes again. It was beautiful. Horse and rider were as one, a singular movement, a silent conversation that no one else could hear. Char found herself instantly enraptured by the beauty, the athleticism, and the bond that horse and rider shared. It was amazing to behold. Char stood safely beyond the gate, watching and unseen, until the car that had come up behind her honked, and startled her back into reality. Her trance was broken, and she climbed back in her car and drove through the gate.

Her heart was pounding but she didn't want to let on about her feelings, so she followed the plan. She kept her head down. She went about her business. First, she checked on Mystic and gave him a once-over. Good. She then grabbed his halter and led him to the lower pasture so he could run around and play, out of the four walls that were his stall. After releasing him to prance and roll and race about, she walked back to the barn and found his bucket and filled it with a scoop and a half of grain. She was just leaving the barn again to go down and watch him when Petra and Erde walked into the barn, having just finished their ride.

"Hello, Char," Petra said politely, perhaps a tad reserved. "You missed your lesson yesterday."

"Did I?" Char honestly hadn't intended to be a flake. With everything going on she must have spaced it entirely. She was genuinely embarrassed about standing Petra up. "Please forgive me, I don't know where my mind has been lately. I will pay you for the time. I'm sorry, Petra."

"Don't worry," Petra said, standing at the entrance of the barn. Between the three of them, Petra, Erde, and Char, the entrance to the barn was blocked off and no one could pass through. Jose had just pulled up with a wheelbarrow of fresh shavings, and, not wanting to be heard, Petra and Char kept moving, leaving their conversation unfinished. Char continued down to the pasture where Mystic was now happily grazing on some grass, secretly hoping that Petra would meet her down there as she had done before.

Char waited for at least 20 minutes for Petra to show up, but after 20 minutes she hadn't. Growing more desperate than she had imagined she would, Char took out her cell phone and texted Petra.

"Can you talk? I'm down in the pasture."

Silence.

Char began to worry. Perhaps Petra had changed her mind, and decided she didn't want any complications. She stood there for another few moments before checking her phone again. Nothing. Her heart fell as she realized the depth of her feelings for Petra. What started out as a fascination with this world-class rider from Europe had quickly turned into unbridled feelings of something much more. Feelings that were so intense that she couldn't turn them off, couldn't stop thinking about her, a feeling that she wanted desperately to be a part of her world.

"Hey there," Petra's voice called from the edge of the pasture, about 10 feet behind where Char and Mystic were now standing.

This time, Char was the one who didn't want to hold back. She missed Petra. And the time she had away from her over the past few days only made her realize how much she didn't want to be away from her again. Char turned towards the voice and ran as fast as she could on her swollen ankle to Petra. When she reached her, she reached out with both arms and pulled her in close. Petra had an appealing mix of her own fresh scent combined with the smell of the stable mixed into her clothes: one of dirt, sweat, and manure. Char so loved the horses, and maybe Petra, that she breathed it all in fully.

After holding her tightly for some time, Char gently released her and found her way to her lips. She pressed hers against them and grabbed her tight again, kissing her over and over again. It felt so good to be able to express herself. For a minute she wondered why she'd ever tried to hide her feelings. From day one, she realized, there had been something about Petra that she simply loved like she'd loved no other. She was elated to let it out.

"Just because you kissed me doesn't mean I'm not sore at you for missing your lesson and standing me up," Petra said jokingly.

"Oh yeah?" Char said, leaning in one more time. "How about now?" she said, kissing her gently on the corners of her mouth, repeatedly. "Is this working?"

"Nope," Petra laughed, "You are going to have to work a lot harder than that, I am afraid."

Char laughed too.

"Come on," she said finally. "Let's go get Mystic. I need to go bring him back to the barn."

"Okay." Petra agreed. "Char?"

"Yeah?"

"Am I still invited over for dinner with you and your husband?"

"Of course, if you still want to," Char said.

"Of course I do. Why wouldn't I?" Petra then grabbed Char's hand as Char held Mystic by the lead line. The three of them walked, with Char and Petra holding hands, back to the barn.

"I have to go," Petra said. "I have another lesson starting."

"Call me?"

"You bet," Petra said, giving Char a wink. And with that, she let go of her hand, and kissed her sweetly on the lips before heading back to the arena for her next lesson.

Chapter 23

Kim got out of her car and rang the doorbell. Other than a dog barking off in the distance, it was silent. She looked around for a car or person, anyone to let her in, but hers was the only car in the driveway. She decided to try the lock. *Damn!* With nothing else left to do, she walked back to her Mercedes, since it was still hers for the time being anyway, and popped the trunk. She reached inside and dug through the piles of belongings, tennis shoes, riding clothes and saddle, her suitcase, college mementos, and toward the back, under a heap of blankets, a few bottles of good wine. She chose the red one since it didn't need to be chilled, and took it out. There weren't any glasses, but she wasn't in the mood to care, so she checked her glove box for her opener that she always kept for emergencies, as this definitely counted, and walked over to the front steps and sat down. She leaned against the front door as she uncorked the bottle. She took a long, slow swig of the velvety scarlet liquid inside, and relaxed as she felt it warm her insides as it slid down into her stomach. She lifted the bottle and took another swig. It eased the pain a little, but only temporarily. She'd have to continue until she felt numb, as no feeling at all was certainly better than this. She was two-thirds of the way through the bottle when a car pulled up and a handsome man she'd seen maybe once before stepped out of a sexy black sports car. *Was it a BMW M3?* The man got out of the car and walked straight to where Kim was sitting, leaning up against the house, drinking the wine.

"Want some?" she said, holding out the bottle. "I'm sorry I don't have a glass," she said, semi-slurring her words. Before Kent could respond, she'd already informed him, "No one's home. You may as well have a seat and take a swig."

Kent smiled as he walked up to the door and reached over her head to put the key in the lock. He opened the door gently, being careful not to cause her to fall backward into the house.

"Why don't you come in?" he asked, extending his hand to help her up.

"Oh my god," Kim said, still slurring, but now trying to compose herself. "You must be Kent, Char's husband?"

"Last time I checked," Kent said as he helped Kim to her feet. "Come on in. Char should be back any moment. She told me you'd be staying with us for a while."

"Are you sure it's okay?" Kim said. She then started to cry again, and she took Kent's sleeve as he was still holding onto her, and used it to wipe her nose.

Kent looked at the soiled sleeve and blinked a few times, trying to make sure this was really happening. "Uh, yeah, absolutely," he said, feigning delight, "Absofuckinglutely," he muttered as he walked past her and put his briefcase and the day's mail down. "If you don't mind, uh, er, Kim, I'm going to go in and change," he said, holding out his arm awkwardly as if it could infect him lest it came any closer to his body. "Just make yourself comfortable while I go give Char a call."

Kent went into the master bedroom that he shared with Char and took his cell phone out of his pocket. He dialed Char and waited. No answer. He left her a message that Kim was there and in desperate need of a friendly companion, and went in to take a shower. By the time he got out, Kim had wandered her way into the bedroom and was standing there with what little wine was left in the bottle, staring at him.

Kent took two steps out of the shower before realizing that the woman who was in his bedroom wasn't his wife. He froze, staring back at Kim, as the water from the shower continued to run down his naked body and pool around his feet on the slate floor. Without thinking, he grabbed a washcloth that was nearby and held it over himself, a meager attempt to cover his essential parts, which were anything but meager.

Kim was reacting none too fast by this point and took her time trying to drain every last drop from the bottle before realizing that her presence was not wanted here.

"Oh, I'm, I am really sorry," she said slowly. She started to walk toward the slider that led out to the backyard before reorienting herself towards the door that led back into the main room, just off the bedroom. As she turned around to head out the proper way, she tripped on the corner of the bed and fell. (It didn't take much in her current state, as Kim was having a heck of a time just walking before running into the bed.) Poor Kent, a doctor as well as a gentleman, had no choice except to stand over her, naked, and try to help her up. Kent continued to try to hold the washcloth over his genitals, but since he was standing above her it was no use.

Kim stayed on the ground, staring up at the dangling body parts that were hanging in front of her.

"Let's get you up!" Kent said, trying to keep things moving along. He felt embarrassed at unintentionally being seen this way, despite his large endowment, and began to practically drag Kim out of the bedroom.

Did I really suggest to Char that Kim stay here until she got back on her feet? I must have been out of my mind, he thought to himself. This was off to such a horrible start that he wished he'd never suggested it. He vowed right then and there that he'd never shower again alone in his house as long as *that woman* was there.

Chapter 24

It was several hours later before Char finally got home. When she did, she came home to find her husband and Kim sitting in the living room, watching TV and drinking beer. There were cans all over the coffee tables and kitchen countertops, and by the looks of it, they had each had no fewer than about five beers.

"Char!...Char, Char, Char, Char, Char!" Kim stood up ready to hug Char as she came in, lost her balance, and fell back on the couch before trying to stand a second time. "Chaaaar! I love you!" Kim said, hugging Char and hanging on her neck.

"Yes, hi!" Char said, trying to take everything in. She looked over Kim's shoulders and mouthed "*What the fuck?*" to Kent, as she realized she had never seen Kim, or anyone, this drunk before. After hanging on Char for a good three minutes, Char was finally able to remove Kim, who appeared to be acting a lot more like a clinging barnacle than a human at the moment, from her grip. She then went over to greet her husband, who whispered to her that Char may need to keep an eye on her.

"She's had quite a bit tonight," he said. "Anyway, where have you been? This wasn't exactly my vision, to be her babysitter when I said she could stay here for a while!"

"I know, I know," Char said. "I was at Blue Ribbon. I had to go check on Mystic. I hadn't been out there in three days!"

"Three whole days? Wow," Kent said, sarcastically. "How long exactly does it take to check on your horse? Actually, you know what? Never mind," Kent said. "Forget it."

"What's that supposed to mean?" Char asked. "You know I don't have a choice, Kent. I have to take care of my horse."

"You always have a choice," Kent said. " And so do I. And right now, I'm choosing to end this conversation and go to bed." And with that, he got up and left the room.

Char would have to deal with him later. Right now, she had Kim to tend to.

"Come on, Kim," Char said, trying to pull her to a stand. But Kim wouldn't budge. She had already fallen asleep on the couch and was now snoring quite loudly. Char gave up trying to move her into the guest room and instead grabbed a blanket to throw over her. She then turned off the TV and the light and headed in to go to sleep herself.

Fortunately, she wouldn't have to entertain unwanted advances from Kent tonight, as he was angry and kept to his side of the bed. As hard as it had been to bring herself to desire her husband before, it was that much more difficult now that she had developed feelings for someone else. She lay in bed for quite a while, staring up at the ceiling, trying to sort it all out. *What am I going to do?* she thought silently to herself. This was a huge dilemma, and with Kim going through a crisis of her own, she definitely wouldn't be able to discuss it with her. In fact, she had never seen Kim such a mess before. Char thought about how funny it had been but doubted that Kim would be able to see the humor of tonight's drunkenness in the same way that Char had. Perhaps in a few more years when all of this was behind her. Until then...

Char tried her best to redirect her thoughts to her own situation. Since she couldn't discuss the matter with Kent, at least not yet, and Kim was in no position to be a good ear, she thought that she would perhaps reach out to Valerie, that is if she had quit laughing from the last conversation they'd had. At least someone was happy, anyway! Char had just begun to relax, and her eyes were slowly closing when the sensation of her cell phone vibrating on the nightstand startled her back into reality. She had a text, from Petra.

"Wish you were here with me," it said. "When will I see you again?" Char put her phone under the covers so the light wouldn't wake her husband.

"Look who is forgetting my lesson now," she typed, "See you tomorrow at 10. Unless you are canceling?"

"No way, Jose!" Petra texted back. "Look how American I sound!"

"Actually, you sound like you are Hispanic," Char responded. "But that's okay. Good night!"

Chapter 25

By the time Char woke up the next morning, Kent had left for work, but Kim was still sacked out on the couch, limbs falling off the sides, her mouth open to breathe as her nose was amply stuffed. Char doubted that Kim would be in any condition to ride today, so she left out some coffee and a note, and tiptoed out the door. She wasn't sure if she was more excited to have another lesson on Mystic, or an opportunity to see Petra. She decided that having a lesson with Petra was just about as good as it gets.

"Morning!" Char greeted Petra cheerfully as she pulled up to park alongside the arena. As usual, Petra was already inside, lounging one of the horses and getting a jump start on her day.

"Good morning," Petra smiled at Char, giving her the once-over followed by a nod of approval. Just seeing that look that Petra gave her made the butterflies in Char's stomach flutter about.

"I'm going to get Mystic groomed and his tack on, and then I'll be out."

"Take your time," Petra called back. "I'll be here!"

Char entered the barn and passed Jose. She chuckled to herself as she remembered Petra's silly text message, "No way, Jose!", from the night before. She wondered what, if any, dumb jokes like that were common in Germany where Petra had lived.

"Hello, Jose!" she called out, trying not to giggle.

"Buenos dias, ma'am!" he said as he threw a fresh flake of alfalfa into one of the stalls.

Char readied her horse in record time and was just leading him out of the barn when Sue walked in, dressed for a ride herself.

"Char!" she called, "How's Kim? I've been so worried about her!" Although it was tempting for Char to say that she was most likely hungover from the night before, she resisted, not wanting to disgrace her friend during her time of need. Instead, she took the high road.

"You know, it's hard," she said. "She's having a rough go of it."

"I have no doubt of that, dear," Sue said, looking so tenderly at Char. "Hey, since she's staying with you, would you mind giving her a message for me, doll?"

"Of course," Char responded. "What is it?"

"Let her know that she can keep her horse here for the next few months, free of charge. She has enough to worry about right now, and she needs something to keep her going, you know? Tell her that for me, will you dear?"

"Oh, Sue!" was all Char could think of to say. "You are too kind! Yes, of course, I'll let her know! That will make her so happy!"

"All right, dear. Thank you. And you enjoy your lesson!"

"I will, Sue! Thank you! Have a nice ride yourself!"

And with that, Char was out of the barn and walking Mystic up to the gate to enter the arena.

The lesson was grueling as always, and by the end of it, Char wasn't sure who had worked up more of a sweat, her or Mystic. But Char didn't mind; she loved the hard work and really wanted to improve as fast as she possibly could.

"What do you think my chances are for qualifying for the Dressage Championships this year?" she asked.

Petra looked at Char pensively and thought for a moment before responding.

"Sure, it is possible. But it is going to take a lot of work. You are going to have to ride every day and get Mystic into shape. You are going to have to work out too, to be sure you are in top shape. Besides that, there are the tests to memorize, and that will take a lot of effort on your part, both inside and outside of the arena."

"But you could get me there?" Char wanted to know.

"Yes, of course. That is what I am trained to do. That is why they call me 'the trainer'. Now, when are you going to do something for me?" she added.

"Okay, what is it you want exactly?" Char asked.

"I want you to invite me over for dinner," Petra stated simply.

"Okay, but why do you want to come over so badly?"

"Because," Petra said, "I want to meet your husband. Check out my competition."

There was a twinkle in her eye and a smile on her lips as she said this, to which Char replied, "Petra, he's not your competition!"

"Is that so? Good! Because I never lose."

Char wasn't sure whether to take that as a promise or a threat. Not wanting to know how it was meant, instead, she said, "Besides, you already met him the other day."

"That didn't count," Petra said flatly.

"Ok then, how about tonight? 6 o'clock?"

"Okay," she said.

"Okay," Char repeated. "Tonight then. I'll see you tonight, at 6."

Char was halfway back to the barn with Mystic in tow when she suddenly realized she had Kim at home having a crisis, and Kent at work, not speaking to her.

Great, she thought sarcastically to herself. *This ought to be loads of fun...* Not wanting to think about it any further, she took care of Mystic and promised herself she'd figure out a way to invite Kim and Kent once she got home. Until then, she would enjoy a few more minutes of solitude with her favorite companion of all, Mystic. After cleaning him up and getting him put away until tomorrow, she waved goodbye to Petra and left, happy to know that she would be seeing her in just a few more hours.

Chapter 26

Char decided that the best course of action for tonight was to not make a big thing of it. Actually, having Petra over for dinner would force Kent to be pleasant, or at least she hoped. By then Kim would have recovered from her night of binge drinking, and the distraction from her personal issues could take a back seat for at least the evening. In the meantime, she decided to sneak off into her bedroom for a bit to give Valerie a call, and hopefully this time Valerie would be serious enough to give her some much-needed advice.

Although Valerie appeared to consider Char's plight more earnestly than she had during the previous call, she still couldn't help her much.

"Remember Sofia, back when you used to live down south before you ditched me for a better life up north?"

"I remember her," Char responded, ignoring the bait Valerie had thrown down to try and make her feel guilty. "What about her?"

"You two were pretty good friends, weren't you? Perhaps you should give her a call, someone you could talk through your feelings with. It couldn't hurt. I didn't know her well," Valerie continued, "but Duke told me that she used to be straight, well into her forties, before she met Katrina and they hooked up. What do you think?"

"Yeah, you're right," Char said. Then, "I don't know why it didn't occur to me to call her. I suppose I got so used to her and Katrina being an item that I had forgotten she had come out, so to speak, more in midlife, like me. I mean, maybe like me. I'm not even sure yet, really."

"Give her a try," Valerie encouraged her. "Perhaps talking to her will be of some help."

"I will. Thanks, friend." And then, almost as an afterthought, "You and Duke still good?"

"Better than ever!" Valerie said enthusiastically.

"I'm glad. Keep me posted, and thanks for the advice, Val!"

"Love ya, friend!" she said in return.

Valerie may have had her shortcomings, but it was times like this that reaffirmed why she and Char had remained so close, even after they'd moved apart. Char was caught up in a daydream, remembering the hospital stay where she'd bumped into Kent, then known only as "Dr. Dreamy" to them, and the bond she and Val had shared, when she heard a quiet knocking at her door.

"Char, you in there?" It was Kim. It was near 3 p.m. and it was the first time the two friends had seen each other since the night before. Kim had a sheepish look about her, quite contrary to her former self only a few days before. It was amazing the difference a few horrific days could make...

Char opened the door and stood staring at her friend. She looked uncharacteristically beat. Her hair was still mussed and she had on the same clothes from the night before. Her normally glowing complexion was pale. Her shoulders slouched and she had a downcast look about her.

"How are you doing, Kim?" Char asked.

Flopping on the bed as if just reaching the bedroom took all her remaining energy reserves, Kim replied, "Not good. Sorry about last night." Her voice trailed off, embarrassed by her behavior during her drunkenness.

"What? Don't give it a second thought!" Char reassured her. "You are entitled! After what Jim did to you? You have nothing to be embarrassed about! Nothing! Okay? So what if you got a little, uh, tipsy last night."

Char knew that "tipsy" was a vast understatement, but she figured reminding her friend that she was "drunk as fuck" wouldn't do much for Kim's overall morale at the moment.

"Thanks, Char," Kim said. "I hope Kent isn't too annoyed with me either."

"No, I don't think so," Char said. "He's spending all of his extra energy being irritated with me. He probably enjoys having someone in the house that he isn't pissed off at. And I'm sure he enjoyed having someone to have a few beers with last night too."

"Where is he, anyway?" Kim asked.

"He's at work. Oh, by the way, Petra will be joining us for dinner tonight. I thought you'd want to know."

"I'm both excited and jealous," Kim confessed.

"Jealous? Because?"

"Because the two of you are certainly becoming really close. Really good friends. And well, she's the new kid in town, so to speak, and she's super cool seeing as she's the trainer and everything, and well, I don't know. I just wish I could be her bestie too!"

"Don't be silly!" Char said, laughing her words off. There was no way in hell that Char was going to share her true feelings for Petra with her. That was far too close to home to be comfortable, for one. All Char would need would be another night where Kim got overly drunk and divulged this information prematurely to Kent. That was a risk she was not willing to take. So instead, she kept things light.

"Oh, great news!" Char just remembered. "I talked to Sue when I was out at the barn this morning. She told me to tell you to not worry about paying your board for the next few months, it's on the house!"

Kim rolled over on the bed and wiped her hands with her eyes, starting to cry again.

"Kim! This was supposed to make you happy, not cry!"

Sniffling, and wiping her nose on her sleeve, Kim looked up and said, "I am happy about that. But I am also just so sad! I still can't believe this is happening, you know? One minute I don't have any financial concerns, and the next, I'm...broke!" With that, she began crying again, this time audibly, as Char froze at the entrance to her bedroom, unsure what to do. She wanted to comfort Kim, but she also had dinner to prepare if Petra was coming over. She still hadn't talked to her husband about dinner tonight, and, well...

"Um, look here, Kim. It's going to be okay," she tried. "Think of it this way, look how lucky you are to have friends who care about you so much. You have a place to stay with possibly the coolest person on the planet..."

A pillow came flying off the bed and hit Char square in the face before falling to the ground at her feet. Her attempt at humor had worked, and Kim hadn't hesitated to follow her lead and lighten the mood.

"Come on," she offered. "Let's go out and I'll prep dinner. You can be the sous chef. And by sous chef," Char continued, "I mean you will pretty much sit at the counter sipping on cocktails watching me cook. Okay?"

Kim grinned a little bit and rolled off the bed and walked over to Char.

"Thank you. I love you."

"I love you too," Char said. "Come on, it's five o'clock somewhere," she said.

Chapter 27

Char was just about finished chopping the bell peppers and onion for the fajitas they were going to have for dinner as Kim sat on the barstool that overlooked the kitchen. She was just about finished with her margarita when the doorbell rang.

"Would you mind grabbing that?" Char asked, her hands covered in raw chicken.

Kim put down what was left of her margarita onto the counter and walked over to the door. Petra was standing there looking clean and comfortable in blue jeans and a button-down shirt. As usual, she had on a bright smile and held a bottle of wine as her contribution to the evening. She didn't know why, but Kim noticed that Petra's eyes seemed to land past her and on Char, who was busy behind the counter chopping the meat for the fajitas. Kim turned around to see what Petra had fixated on, but as nothing was out of the ordinary turned back and took the wine bottle from Petra, welcoming her in.

"I'm sorry to hear about you and Jim," Petra said in earnest. "So sad. I know that you are staying here for the time being and that Sue isn't charging you for board for the next few months, so, I've been thinking, and it's only right that I don't charge you for your lessons, either, at least for the time being," she said.

Kim's eyes welled up with tears again. It seemed these days that they were just below the surface anyway, and it didn't take much for the waterworks to begin flowing. Any small hit of emotion, and boom! There they were, running down her face and she'd be sobbing all over again. When she finally recovered from the unexpected act of kindness yet again, all she could say was, "Really? Thank you so much. I just can't believe everything everyone has done for me." She then held up her margarita glass in one hand and the wine bottle in the other, as if to silently ask Petra which she preferred. Petra still fixated on Char, momentarily focused on the bottle of wine, pointed to it, and then returned her focus back to Char.

"Char, good evening," Petra stated, rather formally. "Where's Kent? I thought he was going to be here tonight so I could meet him?"

How was she always so damn comfortable? Char asked herself. Just having Petra in her house, after everything that had been going on...the kiss that they had shared the night Petra had come for dinner, the kiss down by the lower horse pasture, and now to have her in her house, where her husband would walk in at any moment, made her nervous as ever. Before Kim even had the chance to ask Char what she wanted to drink, Char was already putting in her request.

"Pour me a glass too, while you're at it, will you?" she said.

"Two glasses of chardonnay coming right up," Kim replied graciously.

Just then the front door opened and Kent came home. Kim tried not to remember last night when she'd fallen and he had just come out of the shower, naked. She hoped to avoid further embarrassment if she didn't let on anything.

"Yep, last night was quite a blur," she said out loud and out of nowhere.

Petra and Char exchanged looks, having no idea where that comment came from. Kent, on the other hand, pretended not to hear and continued on into the bedroom to change out of his work clothes, not even stopping to properly greet the three ladies that were hovering in his kitchen.

"Awkward," Kim muttered under her breath. She hoped she hadn't said it loud enough for anyone else to hear.

As the evening rolled on and the drinks kept going down, everyone began to loosen up and have a good time. By the time dinner was served, the four of them had sat down at the dining room table and had just begun to eat when Char felt something brush up against her leg. She looked up at everyone around the table to make sure that no one had "accidentally" brushed up against her when she felt Petra's eyes boring into her own. The "bump" that she had initially felt now lingered, beginning at her ankle and working its way up her calf and towards the back of her knee, where it slowly began its tantalizing retreat back down around her ankle. This continued several times with Petra's eyes locked onto hers, a slight smile formed on Petra's lips.

"Can I get anyone anything else?" Char jumped up from her chair, escaping the contact. It wasn't that she didn't like it; she did. The problem was that she liked it more than she should, and with her husband sitting right next to her, she worried that things would end badly if she didn't remove herself...immediately.

Kim and Kent, who had been immersed in conversation, looked up in confusion when they saw Char standing at the table. Apparently, they hadn't heard her offer to bring people more from the kitchen and were staring at her quizzically when she quickly raised her glass to a toast.

"To Petra," she said. Everyone raised their glasses. Char sat back down. It was a quick recovery, and she was proud of herself for thinking quickly on her feet, literally. She sat back down, this time with her feet far behind her, hoping that she could evade contact with any other wandering legs or feet throughout the remainder of the dinner. Besides, Char had some serious thinking to do, and she still hadn't had a chance to catch up with Sofia. Although she felt pretty darn sure by this point that she was definitely heading down the same road that her good friend had when she fell for her female boss after being straight for 40 years. *Go figure.*

The rest of the evening went pretty smoothly. Char felt relieved that it seemed to go without a hitch. Petra said goodnight and left. Char made sure to most definitely not walk her to her car. After that, Kent and Char retreated to their bedroom while Kim took to the guest room. As Char lay in bed and tried to fall asleep, she could hear the sound of Kim snoring from the next room. She looked over at Kent, who had fallen asleep too. Char let out a big sigh and rolled over, placing her pillow over her head. She closed her eyes and fell asleep, dreaming of the horses and Petra, as she had done for several nights in a row.

Chapter 28

The morning started out pretty much like most mornings. Char opened her eyes a little after 6 and rolled over. When she saw that the other side of the bed was empty, she didn't think too much about it, except that, as usual, Kent must have awoken before her and was either in the kitchen getting breakfast or had already left for the hospital. She lay stretched out in bed for a few more minutes before willing herself to step out onto the cold floor below. She thought about waking Kim up to see if she wanted to head out to the barn with her this morning, then changed her mind, thinking her friend might need a few more days to recover. She'd ask her tonight if she wanted to go out to Blue Ribbon tomorrow.

Char didn't waste any time getting dressed, but she tiptoed around as she didn't want to wake Kim. She poured her coffee into her thermos, grabbed some peanut butter toast, and headed into the garage to leave. That's when it hit her. Kent's car was still parked next to hers.

Char froze. She froze as the thought crept through her mind, slowly. *Nah...* she whispered. But she still couldn't move. Her mind was racing, searching desperately for another possibility. *Where the hell could he be?* Two more minutes must have passed by, and she still couldn't make herself move. She didn't want to be imagining this nightmare. It couldn't be. But then, suddenly, as if she couldn't take the suspense any longer, her hands let go of the thermos she was holding and she ran back into the house as fast as she could. Hot coffee spilled all over the garage floor. It splashed on her car, hitting the door before landing on the smooth concrete of the garage floor. She almost slipped as she frantically ran back into the house as fast as she could, barely tripping on the step that led up to the door inside. Char flung open the door, harder than necessary, and it ricocheted against the wall before slamming back behind her. By then she was in the guest bedroom, gasping for air. She felt her heart pounding harder than it ever had. Her face was hot and she began to sweat. Panting at the door, she stared at the guest bed in complete surprise. She'd found her husband. And he was in bed. With Kim.

Chapter 29

Char didn't even remember getting into her car and driving out to the barn. She had been sobbing the entire way, trying to reach Petra on her cell as she drove as fast as she could, in and out of traffic, and on top of everyone's bumper who got in front of her. She could barely see, she was crying so hard. And part of her didn't care when she got to the intersection and the lights were so blurry from her tears that it was hard to tell if it was her turn to go.

"Fuck you!" she yelled to the universe, stepping on the gas and flooring it through the intersection. "Fuck, fuck, fuck, fuck, fuck! And fuck you, Kent! And fuck you too, Kim! You fucking goddamn whore of a bitch!" Char pounded on the steering wheel with her fists. She looked over and saw an old man at a stop in the lane next to her. "What are you looking at?" she yelled at him, seething, knowing he wouldn't hear her through her window. She didn't care. She was pissed. And she hated everyone. Everyone that was, except Petra.

Thank God I have her! she thought, still pissed as could be. *What...the...fuck!* She still couldn't believe this bullshit! How dare he? Forget him, the asshole, how could she? After everything, I've done for her! Perhaps I should have told her that she was welcome to borrow everything in my house, "EXCEPT MY HUSBAND!" she yelled.

When Char finally got to Blue Ribbon, she pulled up just as fast as she could, got out, shoved the gate open, got back in her car, slammed the door, and screeched to a stop just inside the gate.

"Damnit!" she yelled.

Petra was on top of one of the younger horses, hoping to get him out for a bit of training while the morning was still quiet. There would be fewer distractions and less potential for him to blow up, as younger, green horses, often did. *So much for that plan,* Petra thought, as she watched Char storm over to the arena.

"Everything okay?" Petra called out.

"No!" Char yelled, as emphatically as she could to make her point. "Everything is not fucking okay!"

Petra dismounted from her young gelding and removed the reins and saddle, allowing him to safely walk and roll about the arena while she talked to Char.

"Whatever happened?" she asked incredulously.

Char, now in a place of comfort, fell into Petra's outstretched arms without hesitation. She was so upset she was beyond caring. She'd lost all her inhibitions because right now nothing mattered other than she needed comfort. And she had come to the first place that she thought of. Petra stood in silence holding Char. Char was crying too loudly for her to speak. She glanced behind Char's quivering back and saw Sue running down to make sure no one had gotten hurt. As Sue approached, she could see that no one was hurt, at least not physically anyway. It wasn't uncommon around the barn and training horses for there to be injuries. But lately, it seemed as though most of the pain occurring around Blue Ribbon was more of an emotional, rather than physical, nature. Sue couldn't help but think that at least emotional trauma wouldn't raise her already sky-high insurance rates the way multiple physical injuries would. With a sigh of relief, Sue motioned to Petra that she'd be up at the house if anyone needed her. She didn't want to intrude, and she'd noticed that it hadn't taken long for Petra and Char to become quite close.

"Char, look at me," Petra said firmly. "You've got to tell me. What has happened?"

Char collapsed to the soft ground below her that was covered in freshly mowed grass. She still couldn't believe it, but there it was.

"I woke up this morning," she began, "and I couldn't find Kent anywhere." A few more tears fell and she wiped them on the bottom of her shirt before proceeding. "I thought he had gone to work, but when I got into the garage to leave for the barn, his car was still there!"

Petra gasped and covered her mouth, waiting breathlessly. She had been at Char's house for dinner only last night, and her mind instantly fell to Kim.

"No, don't tell me," Petra said, putting two and two together.

"Yes, Petra! I knew instantly. When I saw his car still in the garage, I ran through all the places I'd been in the house this morning. There was only one place he could be. I ran inside into the guest bedroom, and, and..." Char couldn't get the words out. She fell over onto Petra's lap, who was now sitting down beside her, her arm across her shoulders. "They were in bed! I was so upset that I don't even remember if I said anything, I just ran to my car and drove here!"

Char continued to cry, aware that her tears were soaking the midsection of Petra's shirt where she was hunched over on her, sobbing. She noticed it but didn't care. She continued to cry, her nose dispensing as much moisture as her eyes. By now her head hurt and her eyes were already growing puffy. She didn't care what happened anymore. She couldn't think beyond sitting here on the grass in Petra's arms.

Chapter 30

The sun was setting and there was a chill in the air. The sky above was a soft gray with pink rays interspersed. Char had no idea how long she'd been sitting outside, crying and holding on to Petra, alternating between closing her eyes to block them from the setting sun which was burning them more, and letting her mind drift far away. She hadn't wanted to let go of Petra, who was the most comforting to her in her time of need. Once Char had wrapped her arms around her waist and buried her face in her lap, she refused to move. And Petra didn't even try to move her, not until the sun began to set and the chill air began to create little dimples down her arms, the fine blonde hairs on them standing up in protest to the cold.

"Come on," Petra nudged her gently. "Let's go inside. It's cold out here, and it's also getting dark."

Char's entire body was so drained from the day's events that she found it difficult to stand. Her head was pounding, her eyes were burning despite the sun having left, and the muscles in her body seemed to have escaped beneath her into the ground below. Petra had to lift her to her feet by reaching around her waist and lifting her up, using her own body to support Char's weight. Petra maneuvered one of Char's arms over her own neck, which provided more leverage to move Char. Although her body seemed to protest every bit of energy expended in movement, Char herself had no desire to protest when Petra took off her shoes and placed her gently in her little twin bed for the night.

The inside of Petra's studio was cramped, and Petra began rifling through her mini-fridge, determining what to eat for dinner, when she heard a knock at the door. It was Sue, holding a pot on top of an oven mitt that was placed over her hand. Steam rose from the warm pot and filled the air with the sweet smell of chili. Without a word, Sue glanced over to the little bed that was in the corner of the room and looked at Char, who was now sound asleep. She handed the warm pot over to Petra, who accepted it gratefully. Sue smiled, backed out of the little room, and went back out into the cold night air, presumably back to the main house.

There was one little desk with a single chair next to the bed, and Petra pulled it out and sat down to eat a bowl of the steaming chili. She ate slowly, never taking her eyes off Char, who even in her sleep appeared to be uneasy. Her face was tight and her lips would purse, and incomprehensible noises that sounded like sobs escaped from her mouth from time to time. Petra wished there was more she could do.

Petra looked at her watch and saw that it was only 7:30 p.m. Although she typically went to bed early in order to be up before dawn to start her day prepping the horses, even this was a bit much for her. However, sitting in her chair, and looking around at the cramped room, she considered her options. She knew she could go upstairs and watch TV with Sue and Joe, but dismissed the idea because she didn't want to leave Char's side. She looked at the little TV in the corner of her own bedroom but decided against turning it on because she didn't want to disturb Char. Finally, with few other options to consider, Petra stripped out of her clothes from the day except for her underwear. She threw on a nightshirt and gently slid in under the covers and next to Char. Char stirred briefly, muttered something incomprehensible, and rolled over on top of Petra, who was lying flat on her back. Without opening her eyes, Char snuggled up close as she had done outside, and flung her right arm across Petra's body, grasping her shoulder. Her face snuggled into the soft crook of her shoulder, and she looked so content now that Petra dared not move a muscle. Rather, Petra took her free hand and draped it across Char gently. She then closed her eyes and drifted off to sleep, more content than she had been in a long, long time.

Chapter 31

Kent woke up early the next morning plagued with guilt. By the looks of it, Char had already left early for the barn. *Good,* he thought. He hoped that Char had been so focused on getting out early that she hadn't noticed his "disappearance". He grabbed his clothes and hopped in the car. He'd shower at the hospital once he arrived. Suddenly, he was eager to get out of the house, and away from Kim. He needed space to clear his head and figure out some things. Mainly, what had happened and what to do next. *What do I want?* Right now he wasn't sure. He loved Char, but he was tired of feeling like nothing more than an ATM machine. It seemed to him that as long as he provided Char with the lifestyle she'd grown accustomed to, she really didn't need him for much else. She was usually gone at the barn with her horse friends, leaving him to his own devices more often than not. Or, on the rare occasions he'd wanted sex, she'd made it feel like some sort of a chore. *It wasn't that long ago,* he remembered fondly, *that she and several of the women at the hospital had given me the nickname Dr. Dreamy.* He looked at his reflection in the mirror of his locker inside the men's room at the hospital, and he honestly didn't think he had aged that much. If he were being honest with himself, he thought he still looked pretty good. He couldn't figure out why his wife no longer appeared interested in him in *that* way. *Still,* he reasoned, *that was no excuse to jump in bed with the first vulnerable woman who happened to be sleeping unaccompanied at my house.*

Kent hopped into the shower and tried to redirect his mind to the day ahead. But as he lathered himself up, he couldn't help but remember that Kim's own hands had caressed the very body parts that he was now scrubbing only hours before. It had felt so incredibly good. And Kim had made him feel as though it had been anything but a chore for her to please him in the way that she did. He was torn. He hadn't forgotten that he was married. At the same time, he had his needs too. And putting it frankly, they had not been met in a long time. He desperately wanted Char to think of him as Dr. Dreamy again but grew more and more worried that that ship had possibly sailed. If the ship hadn't left port already, it certainly would as soon as Char found out about his midnight rendezvous with Kim last night. Kent looked down at himself and could see that he was growing aroused just thinking about last night again. *Shit!* he said to himself. *I'm at work, for Pete's sake! I can't be getting a hard-on when I'm about to go see patients!* As Kent was powerless to stop his mind, and imagination, from taking him back to last night, there was only one thing left to do. He reached up to the shower handle and deliberately turned it to cold. Within seconds his entire body was shivering uncontrollably and he was utterly miserable. He looked down and noticed he was shrinking again. *Thank God,* he thought. Having successfully finished his shower as well as the untimely daydreaming, he stepped out and grabbed his towel. Several minutes later, he was dressed in his scrubs and on his way to his first surgery for the day, all thoughts of both women thankfully behind him, at least for the time being.

Meanwhile, back at the house, Kim wandered around from room to room, for once not entirely sure what to do with herself. *Okay, this is awkward,* she thought to herself. *Here I am in my best friend's house all by myself. I just screwed her husband and now he's left for work and she's not here either.* Kim sat down on the couch and stared out the window for some time, trying to figure out where to go and what to do. She no longer felt comfortable staying there any longer. How could she face Char? And what about Kent? He hadn't even said goodbye or anything when he left for work this morning. Kim put her head in her hands and tried to contain her tears. She was so tired of crying that she attempted to hold it in, but couldn't. It just seemed that each day had brought her more and more bad news along with bad decisions. After contemplating her options for housing, she finally got dressed and packed up her things. She had no idea where to go. All she knew was that she couldn't stay here. She didn't know when Char or Kent would be home, and she didn't want to be here to face whatever anger or rage they may have when either got home. She stood by the front door, ready to leave. She looked around to make sure she hadn't left anything behind, other than her pride and self-esteem. *Too late to get those back,* she thought. Then, as an afterthought, *fuck it,* she said to herself as she swiped several bottles of wine from the table to take with her. *They were already going to hate me,* she decided, *so at this point, I might as well take what I need.* Kim loaded her belongings and the extra bottles of wine into her Mercedes. She started the engine, and just like that, she was gone.

Chapter 32

The sun shone brightly into the little room where Char was still sleeping in the twin bed. The ray of light that hit her eyes caused her to squint as she opened them slightly, trying to remember what had happened. As she looked around, the events of yesterday flooded back to her. She knew she was in Petra's bed, even though she barely remembered how she got there. Mainly she remembered the shock of yesterday morning, when she had realized Kent was nowhere to be found, and the horrible discovery when she did find him.

Char lay in bed for a few more moments, enjoying the sunny little room that she was in, the rays beaming in through the window above her and casting their light on the desk and wall on the other side of the room. It was definitely tight in there, but not too bad for one person, she thought. As Char lay in Petra's bed, she enjoyed being comforted by the floral smell of the sheets that she had pulled tight around her. However, she began to miss Petra already, and so after a few moments she pulled the covers down and sat up in bed, looking for her shoes. She headed outside and walked the few yards down to where the covered arena was below. It felt like a spring morning with the bright sun and dewy wet grass that bent under her weight as she traipsed across it to the arena. She looked up at the beautiful sight that was Petra, riding gracefully around the arena on one of the imported warmbloods that she had brought over from Germany.

Immersed in her training, it took Petra a while to notice Char. When she finally did, a smile as bright as her eyes directed itself at Char, making her wish she could erase all of the drama she'd left behind. Petra rode her horse over to the side of the arena and stopped along the railing where Char was enjoying the performance.

"Good morning," Petra smiled. Last night had been the first time they'd slept in the same bed together. Although nothing sexual had taken place due to Char's traumatic day, it had been an intimate and new experience for them all the same, particularly in the undersized twin bed.

"Good morning," Char smiled back meekly. She wasn't her usual upbeat self, but the smile that crept across her face was genuine. Petra took this as a fabulous sign in light of it having only been 24 hours since Char had discovered her husband in bed with her best friend.

"I have a few more horses to train today," Petra apologized, "but I should be done around noon and maybe then we can have lunch and catch up?"

"Absolutely." Char wasn't ready to deal with reality yet. In fact, nothing sounded more appealing to her than to grab a chair and take up permanent residence on the side of the arena where she could watch Petra train the horses. She was never tired of it. To have this kind of expertise at her disposal, in front of her, was beyond thrilling. People paid hundreds of dollars to watch horse clinics such as this, and here she was with a front-row seat, all by herself. It was a dream to see. Char didn't know what she enjoyed better, watching the ballet that occurred before her, or admiring that the beautiful rider on top of the horse was quickly becoming her lover. *Yes,* she thought. *I will deal with the drama at home later.* Right now she was too fragile. And besides, she just wanted to soak up the beauty before her.

A few more hours passed by as Char sat in the camping chair outside the arena, watching every move that Petra made within. Her movements and corrections were so subtle, that it looked as though the horse was reading her mind. Her legs sat motionless in the stirrups, back erect and strong, hands connected to the bit without pulling. The dance that she witnessed was so beautiful she sat in awe, wanting to soak in as much of it as she could. When Char's mind did wander back to the terrible event that had transpired yesterday, she quickly forced her focus to return to the present, as she wasn't ready to grapple with it yet. She felt lucky that she had an outlet like this to keep her mind occupied, especially right now. She'd wait to deal with it until she could talk it over with Petra, at lunch.

Chapter 33

The yellow sedan with the black lettering on the side that read "1-800-Flowers" pulled up to the Kelley house and parked. A young teenage boy hopped out with a bouquet of flowers and a card that said "Char" on the front. After ringing the doorbell and waiting at the door for several minutes, he decided to set it down on the step and leave it there. He then got back into his car and drove off.

Kent had already tried calling Char several times and his calls continued to go to voicemail. A day had passed and his wife hadn't come home. He knew then that she knew, even though no words had been spoken. Fortunately, at least, when he'd gotten home from work yesterday, Kim had packed up her things and left, avoiding an awkward situation, to say the least. Still, having never been in this situation before, Kent wasn't sure what his next move should be. He tried calling and delivering flowers. She would have to come home at some point and check in, at least grab some clothing or personal items, right? In the meantime, he would continue to go to work during the day, pretending to his colleagues that everything was perfectly "normal," as it should be. The last thing he wanted to do was to let on that something was off and arouse suspicion. Kent intuitively knew where Char would be, but he didn't want to go there, not yet. There would be too many people around, and if things got ugly...he couldn't bear it. He was not the kind of guy to air his dirty laundry in public, at least not until now, and he wanted to keep it that way.

"Dr. Kelley, report to the B wing. Dr. Kelley, you are needed on the B wing." The overhead intercom interrupted his thoughts. Kent hadn't realized he'd been daydreaming until the loud voice overhead startled him back into the present. He put his game face back on and strutted down the corridor, a doctor on a mission. The thoughts of his personal life would have to wait until a more opportune time.

Meanwhile, back at Blue Ribbon, Char and Petra had walked their horses down to the lower pasture where they could graze freely. There was an added advantage in that this area was more private than the arena up above, and they really wanted some time to talk.

"How are you doing?" Petra said, finally, after both horses had run off to graze and they were sitting on the soft grass, sharing a sandwich that Petra had made from inside her small studio. Char paused before taking a bite, as she needed nourishment. What she had in mind, however, was the kind of sustenance that didn't come from food, but from the comfort of Petra's arms. Char leaned over against Petra, inhaling the mix of perfume and stable smells. Petra's arms and shoulders were strong and welcoming, and Char snuggled in deeper as she felt Petra return her embrace.

"Honestly?" Char asked. "I...don't really know how I feel, exactly. I mean, I loved Kent, still love him, I guess, but I've been confused for a while, you know? I'll admit I loved the lifestyle that he provided for us, but I guess I just never really enjoyed the other aspects of our relationship..." Her voice trailed off. "And now, I've found you, and I just can't help myself. At first, I thought it was infatuation, you being this big elite dressage rider and all. It also didn't hurt that you're practically an international sensation, and I honestly just fell for everything about you. All of it. But now, I'm starting to think that maybe it's more than that. You know? Like maybe I was meant to be with a woman, eh, you, all along. It just feels different."

As Char talked, Petra caressed her back by moving her hand in small circles under her shirt. The soft touch of those amazing hands, the hands that easily maneuvered a 700-pound animal were just as delicate as they traced her spine, and sent shivers up and down her entire body. Her body had never reacted this way under Kent's touch, and he had surgeon's hands. No, somehow, this was...different.

"What does this mean?" she asked, questioning. Char's eyes searched Petra's, hoping she would have the answer. "Am I...gay?" She wanted to know.

Petra's hand stopped circling Char's back. She considered her question and thought carefully before answering.

"I don't know what it means, exactly," Petra said. "But I do know one thing."

"What's that?" Char wanted to know.

"If you are having doubts, if you aren't sure about things, then it is better leaving now than staying forever."

"But isn't marriage supposed to be forever?"

"Ideally, yes. But if you know now, in your heart, and I think you have known for a while that you just don't feel the way you ought to feel about him in your marriage, then it probably is better that you leave now," she said.

Char repeated the words slowly. "It would be better to leave now than to stay forever. Wow. Maybe you're right, Petra. And obviously, I'm not the only one who feels this way, otherwise, he wouldn't have jumped into bed with my best friend so fast, either."

"Besides," Petra said with a sultry tone, staring at Char's lips, "you can't deny that you do have those feelings for me, right?"

Char gulped, unable to speak, but nodded. Petra was so close now she could almost taste her. Within seconds, their lips were locked, and Petra's hands had resumed moving around her back, this time pulling her in closer. Char returned the kiss by leaning in, placing one hand on Petra's inner thigh, and the other in her wavy blond hair. Their lips were hungry and continued searching one another, unable to stop now that they'd started. Petra leaned over Char more, forcing Char onto her back under her weight.

"Oh God," Char uttered in heightened tones. By now she had lost herself in Petra's embrace, and she didn't want it to stop. She knew she had found the lover for her in Petra's embrace, her tenderness, her everything. Not wanting to think about anything else, she abandoned thoughts of her home, of Kim, and the situation that lay before her. She surrendered herself to Petra, as the two continued to explore one another on the soft grass that became their haven for the rest of the afternoon.

Chapter 34

Kim had been driving around in her black Mercedes for hours and still didn't know where to go. The last thing she wanted was to show up at her old house, where surely she would be caught up in the embezzlement scandal that her husband had deftly mishandled and gotten arrested for. She had worked at the company with him, so there was no doubt that the wide net that was cast that she would be caught up in it too. Thanks to him she had no choice but to go on the lam. (*Is that what it's called?* she asked herself. *That thing that fugitives do?*) Anyway, the bottom line was that she had to keep her distance or she may wind up going to jail too. And now she couldn't go back to Char's house. Even if Dr. Dreamy was up for another round tonight, she couldn't risk it with Char possibly being there.

Kim drove around for several more hours, stopping first in a residential neighborhood where she planned to sleep in her car, but then felt weird and drove away. She went to a parking lot but the lights shone super brightly and she didn't feel safe. Finally, with nowhere else to go, she drove her car towards Blue Ribbon stables. At first, she drove past the entrance, trying to check out everything and see who was awake in the main house, how many cars were there, etc. After she got that information, she drove past again and pulled off down the road where her car would not be seen by the likes of Sue and Joe, Petra, Char, or any of the other boarders. It was after 11 p.m. and the street was pitch black, making it difficult to see. Kim turned on the light from her cell phone and searched through the pile of clothes in her trunk for something warm, and a bottle of wine that she'd stashed back there.

She closed the trunk to her car as silently as she could, and walked down the road toward Blue Ribbon. Since she didn't have her car with her, she could avoid the gate at the main entrance, so instead she snuck through into the yard via a small opening on the opposite side of the house that was lined with shrubbery. It was late enough that other than the glow of the television emanating from the living room where Joe or Sue were probably up watching TV, there were no lights. The lights down in the barn had been turned off after Jose had done the feeding for the night, and the barn door at the end had been pulled shut. On the backside of the barn was a huge pile of hay, and Kim decided that this would be the best place for her to sleep tonight. Ordinarily, she would have knocked on Sue's door and explained the situation, but in light of her escapades with Char's husband, she thought better of it. She didn't know what Char had shared with everyone, and was too afraid to find out. Instead, she decided to lay low for a while. Sleeping in the hay barn felt like the safest place for her to be until she could come up with a better plan.

Having been accustomed to luxurious accommodations since her business with Jim had been so lucrative, sleeping outside in the hay was certainly a stretch. However, Kim was extremely tired by now and didn't want to arouse suspicion, so she wasted no time laying down in the hay where she could close her eyes and rest. She forgot about the wine that she had stuffed in her coat as soon as she stumbled into her makeshift "bed". The cool night air washed over her, and the soft pawing of horses and their occasional whinnies put her at peace. There was something about being out here, away from the hustle and bustle of urban life, that did her soul some good. *It's a good thing I like it,* she thought, *as I may just have to get used to it.* The sound of a barking dog off in the distance, combined with a lone cricket somewhere in the barn, worked in concert to lull Kim to sleep. Her thoughts and worries would be saved for another day.

Chapter 35

With each passing hour, Char felt more certain that she knew what she needed to do. As much as she had wanted it to be, her heart just wasn't in her marriage. *And by the looks of it,* she thought sarcastically, *neither was Kent's.* The only thing Char thought was working for Kent had seemed to be his dick. And now that he'd used it on another woman, it had made Char's decision that much easier.

Although she was beginning to gain some clarity, especially now that she'd had another perfect sleep snuggled warmly in Petra's arms all night, she still wasn't ready to do anything drastic or rash.

"Let everything settle in for a while," Petra had suggested.

"Yes, that's a good idea," Char agreed.

They were still basking in the rare opportunity that Char had to be in bed with Petra, not rushing to start their day, when they both heard a shrill scream. Since they were surrounded by young and powerful horses, accidents and injuries were never far from anyone's thoughts. Without thinking, Petra and Char scrambled out of the small bed, nearly tripping over one another, and ran out as fast as they could to where they had heard the scream. Within seconds, they heard it again.

"It's coming from behind the barn!" Petra's eyes were frantic as they searched Char's for answers. "Maybe there's an intruder! Come on!" she yelled, running towards the sound. The two women rushed down as fast as they could, rounding the corner at the end of the barn and heading towards the hay barn where they had heard the screams. They came to a screeching halt when they saw Jose standing near the pile of fresh hay with a pitchfork aimed at something rustling in the haystack. All three of them looked quizzically at one another, now more confused than scared, until finally, an arm poked out from below the pile to brush off a few pieces from across her face.

It was undeniably, unequivocally, and inexcusably...Kim!

"Kim?" all three of them shouted at once.

Jose was the first to speak, "Que estas haciendo? What in the world are you doing here?" he asked.

Next, Petra wanted to know, "How long have you been there? Were you there all night?"

Char, suddenly overcome with hatred, unlike anything she'd ever felt before, screamed at the top of her lungs as loud as she could while leaping into the pile of hay that covered Kim. "You slut!" she screamed, "You fucking slut! I can't believe I let you into my house and this is what you do to me! You are a pig! This is where you belong, in the hay with all of the other farm animals..."

As Char continued screaming, she slid on top of Kim and began hitting her as hard as she could. The hay was slippery and Kim tried to get out from under Char but couldn't. She kept throwing more and more hay off her face so she could breathe, only to find herself under another pile as Char changed tactics from fighting to trying to submerge her under the pile. She had clearly lost control.

Jose leaped onto the pile and steadied himself, trying to break up the fight. "Call the police!" he yelled. "They won't stop!"

By now the two women were rolling through the pile of hay, hand over fist, pushing one another, screams emanating from them as they unleashed their fury. Char releasing the anger from her best friend screwing her husband, and Kim from her husband losing everything they had worked for and for being a lying sack of shit. It didn't matter if Char didn't deserve it; she didn't care, she was angry at everyone and everything and besides, it wasn't fair that Char had the perfect husband while Kim had discovered she had married a con man.

The two women continued rolling and fighting their way through the mess of hay, pulling at each other's hair and screaming, neither one backing down. Finally, a voice they both recognized pulled them out of their angry trance and they stopped at once, except for gasping for air as their hearts pumped over time in a desperate attempt to funnel air into their lungs and limbs. It was the man they had both been fighting about, standing before them.

"Kent? What are you doing here?" they said in unison. They looked at each other. Then, returning to their anger, "Shut up, bitch!" Char said. "He's my husband!"

"You can't make me, bitch," was Kim's juvenile reply. The two ladies sounded no more grown-up than a couple of schoolgirls fighting in the sandbox at recess time.

"Hey, Char, sweetheart…" Kent said, his shoulders hunched and his head lowered. Kent looked to the side and said quietly, as if not wanting anyone else to hear. "Can we, uh, talk?"

By now Sue and Joe, who had heard all of the commotion up at the house, had come running down to the barn as well. Joe was carrying a rifle, and Sue was right behind him, attempting to hide by holding onto the back of his shirttail. When the two realized that all of the ruckus was coming from none other than the usual boarders plus one husband, Joe lowered his rifle and looked around, dumbfounded.

"Well I'll be…" he said. "Perhaps it's none of my business, but you all need to learn to get along! Come on Sue," was all he said. He then turned and began walking back up to the house. Ever the busy bee, Sue stayed behind, trying to get an inkling of what was going on.

"Sue!" Joe yelled. "I said come on! Leave these guys alone. They can work out their own problems without our meddling," he said. Reluctantly, Sue followed her husband's orders, walking slowly away from the group. She didn't utter a word.

Petra stepped forward and addressed Kent directly. Even with everything going on, Char admired her confidence to take charge of the situation.

"Kent," she said, "I don't think Char is ready to talk to you just yet." Then, turning to Char, she asked directly, "are you hon?"

"Hon?" Kent interrupted, sounding incredulous. "What the hell is going on here?" he asked, his voice booming. Then directing his words at his wife, he asked, "Char? Is there something going on between you and this…this…this German woman?"

"My name is Petra," she addressed him again, deliberately emphasizing the syllables, "Pe-tra."

"Yeah, yeah," he said, shaking his head. Kent walked off slowly, shrugging. This was too much for him. It was one thing to have a one-night stand, a lapse in judgment, so to speak. But now it appeared as though his wife had some…emotional connection with her trainer? It was too much for him to take in all at once.

As he walked off, Kim stood up and dusted herself off from the hay. She took her hands and tried to straighten her hair, clearly used to being the object of attention.

"Kent, wait!" she called, running after him. "Hold on, I'm coming…"

Petra leaned into the pile of hay that now looked more like a disaster than a pile. She reached her hand forward to pull Char up, but Char, unexpectedly playful, pulled her down into the pile with her. They were quiet as they heard Kim, now halfway up the hill toward the entrance, yelling after Kent.

"Wait, Kent! I have nowhere to go..." She sounded so desperate that Petra and Char couldn't help laughing. They laid back in the hay, laughing and laughing while tears streamed down their faces. It was a welcome release after the stressful start to the day. Finally, they stopped laughing. Petra's face turned serious and she stared intently into Char's eyes.

"You okay?" she asked.

"Yeah, I think so," Char said, suddenly feeling much better. She too grew serious and leaned in to kiss Petra. The touch of Petra's lips on hers was medicinal, healing everything that ached inside her. Suddenly, Char felt as though her life was finally beginning to make sense. The way she felt when she was with Petra, and everything they had in common. *No,* she thought. She just couldn't go back to Kent, no matter how nicely he had treated her. *Present betrayal excluded*, she thought, thinking of Kim.

"Come on," Petra said, trying once again to pull Char up out of the hay. "Let's get you back to my place. We'll have some coffee, and start this morning again."

Char was beaming. Nothing sounded better to her than coffee, Petra, and starting over.

Chapter 36

The flowers that had been delivered two days before were still sitting on the front porch when Kent arrived. He picked them up and dropped them into the garbage can under the sink. He opened the refrigerator and stood in front of it. He was out of beer. *Serves me right,* he muttered to himself. He needed a drink. Had to have a drink. He opened up the cupboard and saw an old bottle of half-used whiskey. Reaching for it, Kent pulled the bottle down, pulled off the cap, and took a long and gratifying swig.

"Aaaah..." he sighed, feeling the warm liquid run down his veins and into his belly. He was feeling unmotivated to do anything at all. He was drained emotionally as well as physically. Kent picked up the remote and clicked on the TV, taking another swig of the whiskey. He hadn't bothered to measure it in a shot glass or whiskey glass, as he was too lazy to get one and didn't care how much he drank anyway. When he first sat down on the couch and was sober, calling Kim for another rendezvous had not seemed like a good idea. Now, for the life of him, he couldn't remember why not. Kent picked up his phone and scrolled through it, trying to find Kim's number. When that didn't work, he went on Facebook, where he found her there. He sent her a direct message.

"Where are you?" His phone beeped as the message was sent.

A few seconds later came the reply.

"In my car. Where else?" His phone beeped again.

Kent knew he was already planning to invite her over, but now he had an excuse.

"I can't let you stay in your car," he responded lamely as if he wasn't already looking for another hookup. "Why don't you come over here?"

"Really? Awesome!" His phone beeped again. "On my way."

Within about 15 minutes there was a knock on the door.

"It's open!" Kent called, too lazy to get up from the couch.

"I brought you something," Kim said, smiling wryly as she held up a dead carnation that had fallen from the bouquet that had been left outside.

"Very funny," he said. Holding up the bottle, he offered her some whiskey. "Want some?"

Kim walked over and took a swig, and settled in beside him on the couch.

"What are we watching?" she asked.

"I dunno. Some crime show I think."

Kim feigned enthusiasm, "Perfect! Did you see Jim on there yet? You know, men who lie to their wives and end up embezzling money from their company, leaving their wives destitute and living in their car? Did that come on yet?"

Kent didn't answer but gave her a sideways glance, and gestured for the bottle. Kim handed it back, giving Kent an opportunity to take another swig.

"Now what?" he asked.

"Beats me, Dr. Dreamy," Kim said, batting her eyes flirtatiously. "But I've never played doctor before."

Kent instantly clutched himself, excited by the mere thought of what she had just suggested. He stood up, and although out of practice, tried his best to banter back.

"Just one moment while I grab my stethoscope," he said, walking into the bedroom.

Within just a few moments he returned, and when he did, he was surprised to see that Kim had already undressed.

"I thought I'd make it easier for you to examine me, doctor," she said, taking another swig from the bottle that now was nearly empty.

Kent threw down the stethoscope and lunged toward her, scooping her up from behind her knees, and carrying her back into the bedroom.

"Ooooh," she played along, swooning. "Where are you taking me?"

"This is a private office visit," he said, feeling her soft skin against his strong hands, as he gently lowered her onto the guestroom bed where they had allowed themselves to cave into temptation only a few nights before.

With his gut full of whiskey and his head cleared of rational thought, Kent began to do what previously would have been unthinkable. Only now his wife had found someone else, and he couldn't think of a reason to deny himself this pleasure any longer. He laid Kim on the bed and eyed her lustfully. When he could take it no more he spent a few minutes on foreplay, mostly for her sake, before deciding he wanted more. He penetrated her, enjoying the sounds and the pleasure that they both derived from it. When it was over and they were both satisfied, he rolled over and fell asleep.

Chapter 37

Petra avoided leaving the little room that had become their sanctuary from the outside world as long as possible. She looked at her watch for the last time and said to Char, "Get some rest, okay? You can stay here as long as you want. We will figure everything out later." She leaned in and wrapped her arms around Char, who felt so content that she wished she could hold on forever. "I have to go," she whispered, kissing her gently on her cheeks and forehead before settling on Char's lips. "Don't go anywhere, okay? When I'm done with my lessons I'll hurry back, and we can discuss our next steps then, all right?"

Reluctantly, Char let go of the strong shoulders and promise of comfort that Petra offered before nodding in agreement. "Bye," she said. "Have a good ride, or lesson, or whatever you're doing. I'll be here when you're done."

With one hand holding the door handle, Petra used her other hand to blow Char a kiss. She gently closed the door behind her and walked down to the arena below, where her next lesson was already circling the arena, warming up her horse.

"Very good!" Char could hear Petra call to the rider as she hurried down to the arena. Char let out a big sigh and looked around the tiny room, wondering what she should do. She didn't feel like watching TV and didn't feel like going to sleep.

I know! she said to herself enthusiastically, dialing Valerie.

"Hello, Char?" said the voice on the other end of the phone. "What's going on? You still got the hots for your German trainer, what's her name, Paula?"

Char rolled her eyes and corrected Valerie. "Petra," she said. "And yes, we still are very much enjoying one another's...company," she hesitated. "But Val, something's happened and I really need to run it by you. You'll never guess what happened!"

Char told Valerie the entire story of how Kim had found out her husband had been embezzling money in their business, and how Char had offered for Kim to stay at her house temporarily until she found a new place to live until she had discovered her own husband next door in the guest room with Kim.

Clearly, Val was stunned. "Val, you still there?" Char asked. Char pulled her phone away from her ear and looked at it to make sure there was still a connection. She faintly heard Valerie on the other end.

"Yeah, I'm here." This time there was no laughter in her voice, unlike the last time when she had found Char's own mishaps around her illicit affair with Petra so hilarious. After a long silence, she finally asked, "What are you going to do?"

"I'm leaving him, obviously," was Char's quick reply.

Valerie wasn't so sure this was such a good idea.

"Are you sure, Char? This is all happening so fast. Perhaps you want to go to counseling, or take some time to think about things, or..."

Char interrupted.

"No, I don't need to take time to think about things. I already know what I want. Besides, if he wanted the marriage so bad too, then he wouldn't have jumped into bed with my best friend the first chance he got," Char replied.

"Hey! I thought I was your best friend!" Valerie said, feigning profound sadness.

"Come on, Val, you know what I mean!" was her friend's only reply.

"Well, okay..." Valerie sounded hesitant. "But, what are you going to do for money? I mean, if you leave Kent, how are you going to pay for your own bills and expenses, let alone those for your horse? I know they cost a small fortune."

Suddenly Char felt self-conscious and didn't have an answer.

"I haven't gotten that far," she mumbled quietly.

There was silence on the other end. Clearly, Valerie was torn between trying to be supportive yet being practical at the same time.

"Well," she said finally, "you know I'm here if you need me."

"I know," Char replied. "Thanks, Val." Then, as an afterthought, "Hey Val?"

"Yeah?"

"When are you going to come visit me? You've never been up north since I moved, and I would really love to see you. Especially right now with everything going on and all. I mean, I could really use a friend..." Char's voice trailed off.

"I know," was Valerie's only response. "No promises, but I'll see what I can do, okay?"

"All right. Thanks, Val. I love you, pal."

"Love you too. I'll call soon. Bye."

"Bye."

Chapter 38

K ent's life was quickly forming into a new and uncomfortable pattern. Go to work. Come home. Tell himself he wasn't calling Kim. Then he'd drink, call Kim, and have sex. He'd wake up the next morning regretting his actions from the night before, so he'd leave the house early, and get to work where he'd start the entire cycle all over again. This routine quickly turned to self-loathing, and the self-loathing would cause him to drink, and the cycle became harder and harder to break. Each day he'd wake up anew, making a vow he'd do this day different than the last, and each time he'd fall right back into the same predictable pattern.

And so it was until one day he was at work when a disruption in his new routine caught him off guard.

"Kent Kelley?" the police officer asked. Kent nodded. "I regret to inform you that you are being served," the uniformed officer said. "Sign here, please."

Not wanting to cause a scene at his place of employment, Kent stepped around the corner away from the main hallway and quickly signed the form that had been placed on top of a clipboard that had been handed to him, with one of those pens that were attached by a long string. He quickly signed his name, which was mostly illegible as were most doctors', and looked briefly back up at the officer before being handed a large manila envelope.

"Thank you," the officer nodded, tipping his hat at Dr. Kelley. "Have a nice day, doctor."

"Yeah, right," he muttered sarcastically to himself. Kent walked back to his office before opening the envelope to see the contents inside. Although he had a hunch as to why he was being served, he still couldn't actually believe it...they were divorce papers, and Char had found an attorney to represent her. He threw the stack of papers on his desk and fell back into his chair, leaning far back and placing both hands over his eyes. He needed a moment. He heard a faint rap outside his door. It was probably one of the station nurses, needing his signature on something.

"Not now!" He yelled louder than he had meant to towards the door, unaware of who was behind it. The door proceeded to open slowly anyway.

"I said...NOT NOW!" Before he could stop himself, the willful individual on the other side of the door had revealed herself, and it was none other than Kim.

"I'm sorry," she said, taking a step backward. "I uh, I'll come back. I didn't mean to disturb you."

Kent's voice softened and he directed her to a chair on the other side of his desk.

"No, no," he said, "I should be the one apologizing, not you. I'm sorry. I, just, uh, wasn't expecting you, that's all. I thought it was one of my many nurses, just bombarding me again. Anyway, what are you doing here?"

Kim felt uneasy but managed a small smile.

"Nothing, really," she said. "I just wanted to surprise you is all. I thought maybe we could go have lunch or something?"

"Lunch, right," he said. Suddenly he realized he hadn't eaten all day, and his stomach was now rumbling in protest inside him. "What time is it anyway?" he asked, looking around for a clock.

"It's 12:30," Kim offered. "Have you," there was a pause, "already eaten?"

"No...no, I haven't." Then, standing up, he said, his mood changing for the better, "Great idea. I could use a bite to eat. What did you have in mind?" he said, escorting her to the door.

Kim and Kent passed by the nurses' station, where Kent's companion didn't go unnoticed by the nurses who were gathered behind the counter. They looked away as soon as they saw him walk by, but as soon as he did, they were already gossiping.

"Did you see that?" one of the nurses asked.

"Yeah, what's going on?" replied another.

The two nurses looked at each other and shrugged their shoulders. One of them admonished him out loud, "Mmmm hmmm," she said. "He should not be doing that."

"Doing what?" A young blonde had just walked up to the station and over-heard the conversation.

"Dr. Kelley," the first nurse said, "He is making some bad choices, yes sir-ree..."

The young blonde shrugged her shoulders and walked off. She had no idea what the other two were talking about. As far as she could tell, Dr. Dreamy was always the subject of some sort of gossip, as all the women wanted him. Not giving it a second thought, she left the station and went about her day.

Chapter 39

Char woke up several hours later, feeling much more refreshed than before she'd gone to sleep. She felt as though her nap gave her a chance to restart her morning and erase the horrible manner in which it had begun. It was a gorgeous spring day outside, and she did not want to waste another second missing out on it by staying inside the little studio, particularly when Petra and her horse were both within reach just beyond.

She rolled out of bed and pulled on a pair of riding breeches, prepared to make the most of her day. There was a banana and some sort of fruit bar lying on top of a desk, and Char chomped them hurriedly before heading down to the barn. By the look as well as the smell of it, Jose had recently finished mowing the grass that grew abundantly outside the covered arena, and Char took a deep breath, inhaling it deeply. She had always loved the smell of freshly cut grass. The warm sun on her back and shoulders felt so good, and she relished being able to be outside today. Char watched Petra riding expertly in the arena on her own horse, Erde, and smiled. It was rare that a trainer actually found time to work on one of her own horses, as the clients' horses were always the priority. Riding your own horse didn't pay the bills either. The hope was that down the road with enough training they could be sold for a hefty amount, but that was years down the line. This is why the immediate needs were always taken care of and the clients' horses came first.

Char could tell that Petra was focused on her training and hadn't noticed as she walked by and headed into the barn. Char didn't want to disturb her, so she kept walking without calling out to say hello or anything.

"Hello, Mystic!" she said, rubbing his soft muzzle. She could tell Mystic enjoyed the attention, as he stretched his head and neck as far as he could out and over the top of the stall half-door and rubbed up against her in return.

Just the size of his head was enough that it could be used as a weapon if he had wanted to. Fortunately, horses seldom were aggressive, and if they were it was usually their hind legs that were the weapon of choice. Char was awed at the connection between human and horse, a silent language of friendship that bonded them to one another. It was truly humbling and magical.

Char put the halter around Mystic's head and led him out of his stall into the usual spot in the barn where she'd hook him up to the cross ties and begin grooming him. She loved everything about being with her horse, including the time to brush and comb him, clean his hooves and curry his forehead. Finally, it was time to put on the saddle, gently so as to not hurt his back, and slowly tighten the girth around his belly. When this was all done, she got out the bridle, being careful not to bang his teeth with the iron bit as she inserted it into his mouth, and led him out to the barn.

Char stood silently outside the arena for a few minutes, as Petra was clearly concentrating on one of her upper-level dressage tests that she was rehearsing for an upcoming competition. She didn't want to interrupt her concentration or get in the way of the prescribed sequence of maneuvers that took place using the entire arena. Besides, she welcomed any opportunity to continue to watch Petra, as she loved not only the sport and the way Petra rode, but she was starting to fall for the rider as well.

At first, Char had been confused by her feelings for Petra. She was 35 now, not even a young adult, and had never had feelings for another woman before. She hadn't even experimented in college, as she had had no desire or attraction to a woman, ever.

And then Petra came along, and she was, well...enamored. At first, she was confused because she thought perhaps she was simply infatuated with the entire image that was Petra, this worldly dressage rider that she had wanted to emulate. She was fascinated by her since she had grown up in Germany and had this marvelous accent. She just seemed so...intriguing.

And then there was the kiss.

That's when Char knew that this was much more than simple international intrigue. The way her body had responded when they had touched, the way she felt when Petra had held her during her time of need, everything about Petra had felt like it completed Char, rather than feeling odd and uncomfortable, the way she imagined it would with any of her female companions. She had no desire to be physically close to any of them, and quite frankly, the mere thought of it had repulsed her. The more she thought about it, the more she became convinced that Petra was "her person," so to speak. She had already been infatuated with horses, a trait that followed in her mother's footsteps. But now that she had Petra here too? There was no place she'd rather be. Her only wish was that she was an expert rider already, then she could make her living riding and selling horses too, instead of wondering what in the world she was going to do now that she had served Kent divorce papers and was setting him free.

It had been a fast decision, but one that Char felt was right. True, she wouldn't have the pampered and easy lifestyle that she had enjoyed up until now, but that was okay. She knew that in order for her to be happy, she needed to live an authentic life. She could never stay with Kent just to use him for the financial lifestyle that he provided. Despite his recent poor decision-making in which he crawled in bed with her best friend, he had been a really nice and supportive husband, always wanting her to be happy. Although she was extremely hurt and disappointed by his actions, she felt partially relieved as well. It was only the beginning of their marriage and already she had hurt him by not wanting to be with him in the intimate way that a marriage deserved. Now that he had taken another partner, and frankly, so had she, they were both free to move on. Char just worried about how she would be able to do that and still be able to afford Mystic and her riding lessons. Even if she could afford to keep Mystic, she reasoned, with a full-time job to support herself there would be no time to come out to ride except on weekends and perhaps after work in the evenings if she was able to find the energy. At least Blue Ribbon had a covered and lighted arena, so she could ride after work in the evenings if she had to. But still, there was now a huge piece of her life that she would have to figure out.

"I'm done, if you want to come in," Petra called to Char, who was still waiting outside the arena. Char snapped back from her reverie, and was suddenly back in the present moment, still standing by the arena gate.

"Thank you," she said as she walked into the arena. "How was your ride?"

"It was good," Petra shared, but then confessed, "if only I could just focus on Erde," she said, patting him on the neck. "We could go so far. Perhaps even qualify for the Dressage Championships this year," she said. "The problem is that he is not my only focus, and in order to pay my bills I have so many other horses to ride and train. There simply are just not enough hours in the day," Petra admitted, before adding, "On the other hand, I am just so lucky to be here and to have this opportunity that I shouldn't complain. It will all work out, right?" she said.

Char admired Petra's optimistic attitude and wished she could look at her own situation with the same positivity. "Right! I need to remember that for my current situation as well!" she agreed.

Petra shot Char a loving look that made her want to melt. "Yes," she continued, "I have been thinking about you...and us, as well. And I have a plan for that too," she said. "A plan that may just help both of us," she said, smiling.

Char lifted her chin up, excited to have someone else come up with an idea, as she was certainly looking for some good options. "Oh?" she asked, clearly intrigued. "Tell me!" she insisted.

"Not now," Petra said, giving a nod to Mystic, who was now standing in a relaxed position with his head hanging about six inches from the ground. "Your horse thinks he's in retirement already!" she laughed. "Come on, there will be time for that later! Right now, we have a lesson to conduct..."

"But I thought you were too busy today? Don't you have other horses to ride today?" Char protested. "I had just planned on riding on my own."

Petra rode Erde close to where Char was standing, so no one else could hear. "Look baby," she said. Char's stomach tingled as she heard the words. Petra had never called her "baby" before, and she liked it. "We're in this together now, you and me. And there's no way in hell that my partner isn't going all the way to the top. I have a reputation to develop in this country, eh? So, I'll go get that other horse that I need to train today, and I will ride while I give you your lesson. In the meantime, you go get warmed up and I'll be back in a few minutes. Okay? I just have to put Erde here away."

Char was so excited she couldn't believe it. She wasn't sure if it was that Petra was going to ensure that Char had all the necessary skills to take her to the top of her riding career, or because she had called her "baby". Either way, the effect her words had on her made her extremely happy.

"Okay! Thank you!" she said, looking around before blowing Petra an imaginary kiss. "I'll get warmed up then!"

Char nudged Mystic with her hips and legs while gathering up her reins, giving him the signal that it was time to go to work. He picked his head up and began to walk forward. Petra was already headed to the gate and out the door to get her next horse.

Char shouted after her. "What about your idea?" she called.

"Later," was all Petra said, as she disappeared into the barn with Erde following eagerly right behind.

Chapter 40

Kent and Kim pulled up to the unfamiliar Chinese hole-in-the-wall off the beaten path, as he didn't want to risk running into anyone from work. Although it was no one's business, he had felt the eyes of the nurses boring a hole into the back of his head as he and Kim had walked out of his office and headed to lunch together. He'd worked with them long enough to know what gossips they were, and the last thing he needed right now was more drama and a potential scandal disrupting his work world, even if he was technically almost divorced.

The lunch started out fine, with Kim ordering vegetable chow mein and Kent ordering kung pao chicken, when Kim began to cry right there at the table.

"I just hate myself right now," she began.

Shit, Kent thought to himself as Kim began to cry. *I was just served divorce papers and now we have to talk about her problems?* But he was trapped in the tiny restaurant with her, so he had no choice but to listen.

Without any prompting, Kim continued her sharing. *She's so overwhelmed she probably would open up to anyone willing to listen,* Kent thought again. He poured them both a cup of the hot tea that always came in those stainless steel teapots and settled himself in, pushing his own thoughts and feelings temporarily to the side. Although Kim's situation wasn't entirely his fault, he knew he at least had some role to play and therefore could at least be there for her.

Up until she had received the news about her husband embezzling all of the business money for their own personal use, Kim had been an upstanding and classy woman. Even Kent had to admit that her actions for the past few weeks were pretty uncharacteristic of her, and he knew it was a result of the unusual amount of stress that Jim had put her under. He couldn't imagine being in her situation, especially considering the scrutiny she was due to face since she had been not only Jim's spouse but an employee of the company as well. It was unbearable just to think about.

Kim was really beginning to meltdown as the chow mein she had ordered arrived, and so the waiter tried his best to be unobtrusive, placing the dish off to the side where her tears wouldn't drip into the fresh plate of vegetables. He took a step back and bowed before dismissing himself without saying a word. Kim didn't seem to notice the food or the waiter and continued crying into her napkin.

"...and to think that I repaid my friend's hospitality by sleeping with her husband!" she wailed. "I had already lost my marriage, my house, my job, and my lifestyle. But due to the generosity of my friends, I was still going to get to keep my horse, have a place to ride, and a roof over my head until I could land on my feet. And what did I do?" She began to cry louder.

In the meantime, another couple had been seated at the table next to them and they were now looking at Kim awkwardly from behind their menus as she continued to carry on, unaware of the volume her voice had now risen to. Kent could feel their awkward glances in their direction, and he gave them an apologetic look that seemed to say "sorry about this." The couple gave a slight nod before redirecting their eyes to their own table and carrying on with the business of ordering.

Kim was just getting to the part where she had woken up at Blue Ribbon after having had nowhere to sleep the night before, and Kent couldn't help but subdue a chuckle that threatened to emerge from his lips if he wasn't careful. Remembering how Kim and his wife had wrestled in the pile of hay was pretty funny, even if it was too soon for anyone else to appreciate it.

"Look," Kent tried his best to reassure her, "you are not the one to blame. Don't forget, I went into your room that first night, not the other way around. If anyone, Char should be angry with me, not you."

Kim looked up at Kent and eased up her tears a bit, but she couldn't completely stop as she continued. "Yes, that's true. But it doesn't matter. After making such a fool of myself the other day by sneaking into Blue Ribbon to sleep...I didn't know where else to go! And I didn't know what was going on with us so I thought I'd better just give you some space. Anyway, I can't show my face over there after that. Char and Petra probably hate me, and I'm sure Sue and Joe aren't too happy either. I'm lucky I didn't get shot, breaking into a barn with show horses of that quality and price! What was I thinking?"

Kent had to admit it wasn't one of her finer moments. Perhaps she had been drinking. He knew he certainly hadn't made many of his wisest decisions while being under the influence; however, being a doctor, he certainly did understand the role that stress can play on the body and on a person's thinking. Kim's behavior had certainly been proof of that.

"Give it some time," Kent said. "I think they'll come around. Besides, as I said, this isn't all your fault. Char has actually moved on too, I'm pretty sure," he said.

Shocked, Kim stopped crying completely this time and looked up at Kent. "What do you mean?"

"Really? You mean you don't know? Char hasn't come home since the night that..." His voice trailed off, not wanting to say it. "You know... Well, anyway, I'm pretty sure I know where Char has been staying."

"Where? Up with Sue and Joe?"

"No. With Petra."

Kim spilled her water all over the remainder of her chow mein. A few ice cubes rolled off the edge of the table and fell onto her lap, leaving wet spots on her pants.

"What?!" she practically screamed, gaining the attention of the couple sitting next to them for the third time. There was now another couple across the restaurant who had also just been seated, and they too gave a sideways glance over at Kent and Kim. This time, Kent couldn't keep quiet.

"Shhh!" he said. "You're getting everyone's attention on us."

Composing herself, Kim finally seemed to notice they weren't the only ones in the restaurant. She looked around, embarrassed, waved "sorry" to the other customers, and lowered her voice this time.

She leaned in. "What are you talking about?"

"I'm talking about Char and Petra," he said in a low whisper, leaning forward as well, trying to make it as difficult as possible for anyone who may still be curious about their conversation to be able to hear what he was saying.

Kim sat silently for several minutes as if she was trying to understand what Kent was implying.

"You mean, Char and Petra are more than just friends?" She said the word "friends" while using her hands to mimic air quotes, putting emphasis on the word.

"Yes, that's what I'm saying," Kent said.

He let the words sink in as Char leaned back in her chair. By now she had definitely stopped crying as she pondered this surprising turn of events.

"Oh my god!" she whispered, trying not to laugh. "Are you kidding me? How do you know?" she said.

"Well...a couple of reasons," Kent continued, looking at his watch. "But I have to get back. Don't forget, I'm still working today, and we've been gone for some time. I really do need to get back. I'll fill you in on everything when we can catch up more, later," he said, signaling to the waiter for the check.

"Oh wow," Kim said, still stunned. Hearing this really had changed her perspective. She was still heartbroken over the betrayal of her husband and felt bad about sleeping with her best friend's husband, but this news...well, it certainly had changed things for her. She still wasn't ready to head back to Blue Ribbon anytime soon, especially after the way she had embarrassed herself and everything, but still. At least now she wasn't feeling quite so terrible... She knew that she now just wanted some time to think, to digest everything that had gone on, and everything she had learned. She thanked Kent for the meal and headed back to her Mercedes, the one thing she still owned besides her horse and her belongings that were crammed into the trunk. She got in her car, and headed, well, she wasn't sure yet. She just knew she was headed somewhere and hoped it would reveal itself as she cleared her head and took the time to just drive and think.

Chapter 41

The day had been long and the sun was already setting by the time Petra finished riding her last horse of the day. She put him away in his stall and threw him some grain before walking the small hike back up to her studio where Char had been waiting. When she walked in, she was surprised to see that Char had dinner ready and had made the small studio not only functional, but had managed to make it a tad romantic as well.

"Dinner!" Char announced proudly, pointing to the desk that had doubled as a dining table for two, covered with an extra bedsheet that now served as a tablecloth. She had even managed to find a candle after rummaging around in a few drawers and had placed it on the center of the table, hoping that Petra would like it. The meal that she had prepared for dinner was all she could find in the cramped refrigerator: a small pepperoni microwaveable pizza and a side salad of lettuce and carrot slices. There was a beer left in Petra's fridge, and Char had opened that and split it between two glasses that sat next to their plates. One side of the table was next to the bed, so that served as a chair. The other chair was the actual desk chair that had been moved across from the table. After giving Petra a minute to look around, Char exclaimed enthusiastically, "Ta-da! Do you like it?"

"It's wonderful," Petra kissed her lovingly on the lips, eyeing the beer that sat on the table. After a hard day working at the stable, she looked forward to having a beer, even if she would need to share hers with Char.

"Thank you for this," she said, genuinely appreciative.

"Sorry it isn't much," Char offered by way of apology. "But hey, you've been to my house before, you know that I can actually cook, right?" she laughed.

"It's great, really!" Petra smiled. "I love it. It's perfect! Thank you. And now," she said, lifting her glass of beer up in a toast, "to us!"

"To us!" Char agreed, raising her glass. Petra drank down her half of the beer and began nibbling on her salad. Char broke the silence, as she had been dying to know all day what Petra's plan had been, the one that she had been too busy to share with her earlier.

"So what's this plan that you've been concocting? The one that you said 'may help both of us'?" Char asked.

Petra paused before answering, as she had now moved on to her pizza and just taken a bite. "Mmm," she said, signaling with her finger that she needed to finish chewing.

"Okay," she said after washing down her bite with the remainder of her beer.

"Well, I was thinking," she began. "Unless you have a plan already in place for what you are going to do..."

"I don't," Char assured her.

"Okay then. Well, you are going to need a job, some way to support yourself, now that you are leaving Kent, correct?"

"Yeah, don't remind me," was all Char replied. "Forget me ever finding time, or the money, to ride again. It'll be just like when I lived in southern California before I moved up here," she said.

"Hold on," Petra said, smiling. "I have an idea for that. You know, you are a pretty decent rider."

"Thank you," Char said, beaming.

"Not fantastic," Petra clarified, "but good. Decent. Anyway, I could use an assistant, someone to..."

Before Char knew what she was doing, she had already flown across the tiny desk and was in Petra's lap, hugging her and kissing her all over her face.

"Hold on a second," Petra said, "I don't know if you are going to be happy with my proposal."

Char paused to listen to the rest of Petra's idea, but she already knew she was going to love it. She didn't care what she had to do, even cleaning stalls would be okay if she had to.

"Suppose we work together. I can't really pay you much if anything right now until I get more established," Petra said.

Char tried not to feel the disappointment. *How was this going to work? Of course, I need some amount of money in order to live...*

"...But I was thinking, I could give you free lessons in exchange for you helping me around the barn. There are always all sorts of odd jobs that need to be done. Jobs that are time-consuming, but would free me up so that I could focus on activities that will boost my career as well as those activities that are profitable. For example, if you could groom and saddle my horses, bring them out and hand them to me, and then you could take them when I'm done, cool them off, and put them away. Bring out the next horse, that sort of thing."

Char was super excited at the prospect. *A job doing what I love! Yes and yes!* She would get to be around horses every day, learning the ropes, growing as a rider, and hanging out at the barn every day...it was a perfect idea! Except for one thing.

"I don't mean to seem ungrateful," she said as her face fell, "but how could I afford that? Yes, it would keep me busy, and I could still have lessons and see you and ride, but where would I live? What would I do for money?"

"Well, that's just it," Petra said, shy for the first time. "I don't know. I mean, my place is very small, but you are welcome to stay here with me until maybe we could get a bigger place?"

Char couldn't believe her ears.

"Petra!" she exclaimed, "Are you serious? Really? This place is itty bitty! It is beyond small. It must be only 35 square feet in here! It doesn't even have a bathroom!"

"I know, I know," Petra said, nodding. "It was just an idea." Her face fell. She had wanted to help out, and she figured they were seldom in the room except to eat and sleep. Petra had been allowed to use the bathroom up in the main house with Sue and Joe, or even the small one down in the barn. But Char was right. It was a dumb idea.

"Yes!" Char shouted, still sitting on Petra's lap and now resuming kissing her all over again. "I love the idea! I could live here with you! We'd be a team! Oh my gosh, I just love it!"

"Really?" Petra asked incredulously. She had already been preparing herself to lose not only time with her new girlfriend (*was that what Char was, her girlfriend?*), but also with a potential business partner as well. Hearing Char's positive reaction was so thrilling! Petra had already thought early on about the possibility of having an assistant, but she couldn't afford to pay anyone at such an early stage of her career. But with Char by her side, the possibilities were endless. She was so excited. There was so much that Char would be able to do for her so that Petra would be able to concentrate on growing her business without burning out. On top of that, she'd get to see Char all the time. This was beyond exciting!

Petra leaned forward and returned Char's kisses, holding her tight and smiling at her for a long time. She gazed into her eyes, so incredibly happy. And then, an unwanted thought entered her consciousness.

"Shit!" she said.

Char blinked, laughing. She'd never heard Petra swear in English before. She giggled at the sound of it, as Petra pronounced it more like "*sheet!*" than "shit". Still, Char regained her composure.

"What's wrong?"

"I didn't think to ask Sue and Joe if it would be okay if you moved in. This is their house, you know. Maybe they won't like it. Or maybe they'll raise my rent. Or maybe they'll just say 'no, you can't do that,' or something terrible like that."

With no time to waste, Char had already jumped up and was pulling Petra outside by the hand.

"Come on!" she said. "There's only one way to find out!" Char had known Sue and Joe for a lot longer than Petra had, and she just knew that her moving in to help wouldn't be a problem. But to make Petra feel better, she had decided it would be necessary to ask anyway.

"Hey, if they say no," Petra laughed, "You can always sneak in at night and sleep in the hay barn! I'll sneak food down to you!"

Char laughed, remembering the morning not long ago when they had woken to Kim, screaming and flailing around in the hay. It had been quite the sight. Char was only just now beginning to find it funny.

"Hey, what about Kim?" Petra asked as they headed up to the Harrisons' front door. "Do you think you two will ever repair your friendship?"

Char took a moment before answering. So much had been going on lately that she hadn't even had time to think about how she felt about Kim after what had happened.

"I don't know," she confessed, knocking on the door to the Harrisons'. "I need some time, I think."

"Fair enough," Petra agreed as the door opened to a smiling and welcoming Sue.

Chapter 42

"Where R U?" Kent texted Kim from the couch, where he'd taken up residence most nights as of late. As usual, the TV and his beer were his constant companions, unless you counted Kim. No response. Kent took another swig of his beer and resumed channel surfing. *If I got any better at this,* he mused, *I could take it up as an Olympic sport.*

Ping... Kent's cell phone got a text back from Kim.

"In your driveway," the text said.

Kent raised his eyebrows. He hadn't heard a car. He got up and walked over to the front door and peered out. Sure enough, there was a black Mercedes parked in the driveway. He texted her back.

"What R U doing?" he texted.

"Waiting." Ping.

"For?" Ping.

"For you to invite me in. LOL." Kim then added a happy face emoji with tears running down.

Kent laughed and got up from the couch again to open the door.

"You're not going to get a more formal invite than this," he shouted, gesturing for her to come in. "Need some help?"

Kim exited the car door and walked up to the house, carrying a hot bag of chicken wings and Ranch dressing that she had picked up at the gas station down the road.

"I brought dinner," she said, not sure if it would pass as such. Then, as an afterthought, "It's still hot."

Kent smiled and took the bag and looked inside. One of the wings was half-eaten and had Ranch dressing smeared across it. He closed the bag back up and gave her a look.

"What?" she said, pretending to be insulted, "I got hungry, okay?"

Kent was too busy dialing on his phone to respond.

"I'd like a large pizza with olives and pepperoni," he said. He put down his phone and turned to Kim, taking her small waist in his arms. "Now," he said, smiling, what about dessert?"

Kim smiled coyly, knowing full well what he meant.

"We haven't even had dinner yet," she stalled.

"So?"

"So? You're a doctor, and your best argument is, 'so'?" she mocked.

Kent thought for a second. Surely he could do better.

"So...it's backward day today," he said. "Meaning, everything is done backwa..."

Kim interrupted him, teasing.

"Yes," she said. "I am aware of what 'backward' means. You don't need to explain it. I just didn't know it was officially 'backward day' today," she exclaimed.

Now it was Kent's turn to stall.

"Well...it's not officially backward day, but, we have 15 minutes until the pizza gets here," he joked, suggesting they start in the bedroom. Just then, the doorbell rang.

"What? I can't believe it! Damn!" he said, opening the door to pay the delivery guy. Kent grabbed the pizza and brought it down to the coffee table to share with Kim.

"So much for 'backward day,'" she teased him.

"Yeah, yeah," Kent played along. "You got me. But it might be 'double dessert day!'" he said cheerily.

"Hold your horses there, big guy," Kim said. "We have some things to discuss still."

"Oh? Like what?"

"Like, what are we doing? What about Char? You, me, where I'm going to live. There's a lot going on right now, Kent," she said. "And we need to do some serious planning. I can't keep driving around in my car like this, trying to figure out where I'm going to stay, what I'm going to do for money."

After a long pause to finish his bite, Kent responded.

"I know," he said casually. "But do we have to figure it all out tonight? Can't we just relax and watch TV, and discuss it later? Perhaps we can talk about it in the morning, when everyone is just a bit more...refreshed?"

Kim thought about it.

"I'm sorry," she said. "You're right, you've had a long day at work, and you're tired. I should be more sensitive to your needs."

"It's okay, doll," he said. "Thank you for understanding. We'll talk about it in the morning, okay?"

Kent and Kim had just settled down on the couch and were snuggling during one of their favorite whodunnit shows when the doorbell rang again. They stared at each other quizzically, with no idea who it was. They certainly weren't expecting anyone this late in the evening, and they hadn't invited anyone over.

Kent rose and peered out the peephole in the front door. He couldn't believe his eyes. Panic shot through him as his adrenaline kicked in and began coursing through his veins. Suddenly he was completely wide awake and felt almost jittery.

"Shit!" he said, panicking. "Quick, you gotta hide!" he announced, dragging Kim into the bedroom by her arm.

Kim followed him into the bedroom, but couldn't understand what could possibly be such a big deal. Who could it possibly be that would have him so worked up?

"It's Jim!" he finally said, whispering in a panicked state as he closed the door behind them, now that they were safely in the bedroom.

The doorbell rang again, followed by a knock.

"Hey, Kim!" The voice carried into the bedroom where Kent and Kim were hiding.

"I know you're in there! Come on out! I want to talk to you!" He waited. Several seconds passed by as Kent and Kim remained frozen in the bedroom, staring wild-eyed at one another as they covered their mouths in horror.

"I see your car, honey! I know you're in there! Come out! I just want to talk." He wasn't giving up, and Kent decided he would have to get rid of him.

"Just a minute!" Kent hollered back from inside the bedroom, where Kim was still standing with a horrified look on her face. Kent motioned to her to stay there, and to lock the door inside the bedroom after he left.

Before she could protest, he was already heading to the front door. Kim shuddered. She didn't know what Jim was capable of. She certainly hadn't had any knowledge that he'd embezzled money into their account. Was he jealous of Kent and coming for revenge? She wanted to run after Kent and stop him from opening the door, but it was too late. Before she could stop him, she heard the door open and close behind him. And then she knew she was completely alone inside the house, with nothing to do but wait.

Chapter 43

It was close to 1 a.m. before Petra and Char finally left the Harrisons' house. There had been so much to tell, and as anticipated, Sue and Joe had been as gracious as ever. When Char and Petra sat down to ask the Harrisons about their plan to work as a team and have Char move in, they had assumed that the rumor mill had been in full operation and that somewhere along the way, Sue had suspected that Char and Petra had become more than just friends with a mutual love of horses. When she finally figured it out, after Char and Petra had to literally spell it out for her, her face had turned a bright pink color and she had just giggled bashfully.

Not knowing what to say, she finally announced, "I guess I'm just a little naive around these matters. Joe and I are old school, you know? I guess my mind just doesn't work in these ways, but if you're happy, then we're happy! Right, Joe?"

"Oh sure." Joe had chimed in from time to time. Although he thought "to each their own" and wouldn't judge, he certainly wasn't comfortable talking about these sorts of things. After all, he was of the generation that didn't allow men to go into the birthing room when their wives were having babies! He was more comfortable waiting outside with a cigar, ready to be smoked as soon as it was over.

"But what about poor Kent?" Sue had asked. She didn't know him well, as he seldom came to any of the barn functions, but Char had never complained about him and she knew he was a doctor. *This would certainly be a lifestyle adjustment for Char*, she thought. Of course, that was none of her business, and so she diverted her attention back to the happy couple.

Char and Petra had conveniently left out the details about how Kent and Kim had hooked up; they figured one bombshell of an announcement in the evening was more than enough for the poor couple to digest. That would have to come later. Besides, it had nothing to do with Char and Petra anyway. At least not really...

With things settled, Char and Petra went back to their tiny room and crammed themselves into the small bed. It was still the "honeymoon" stage of their relationship, so they didn't mind the tight squeeze, but Petra thought she'd better start saving her money for a bigger place now that this was going to be a permanent thing.

The two were just waking up early when Char's phone rang. It was Valerie. Petra knew they would be on the phone for quite a while, and so she kissed Char on the head and walked down to the barn, eager to get a start on her day.

On the other end of the phone, Valerie was already squealing with delight.

"...So in the springtime when I get a week off, I'm going to fly up and see you! How does that sound?"

Char paused. It wasn't that she wasn't excited to see Valerie per se, it was more that she didn't know where she would stay. There was absolutely no more room in Petra's tiny space, and staying at her old house with Kent would be not only unwelcome but awkward. Char regretted telling Val that she'd have to stay in a hotel, but she had no choice.

"Of course I understand!" her sweet friend agreed. "I'm coming to see you! I get it! Besides, I don't want to have to hole up with a couple of lesbians in the same room with me anyway!" she teased.

Char knew her friend well enough to know she was joking and didn't take any offense to her silliness.

"Will Duke be coming?" she asked.

"Unfortunately, he won't. He can't get the time off work right now. Besides, he's more of a surf guy than a horse guy anyway," she laughed. "If he did have extra time, he'd probably want to stay down in Laguna or Newport and catch up on some waves, you know?"

"Well, tell him I said 'hello'," Char said.

"I'll see you soon, Val!"

"Bye!"

Char was so pleased with the way things were going so far. She already had a plan in place, and now her best friend was coming up to support her. Although she'd been happy initially with Kent, it had become more and more apparent as time went on that not only was something missing, but they just didn't seem to have much in common anyway. She had enjoyed a pampered lifestyle before, but now she would have the opportunity to make something of herself and possibly have her own career as a trainer someday. She couldn't believe her good fortune and set outside to tell Petra the good news about Valerie coming to visit. She couldn't wait for her partner and bestie to meet!

Chapter 44

K ent stepped outside and closed the door behind him.

"How can I help you?" he asked. The man was about 5 foot 11. He was quite handsome, Kent had noticed, even if he was a crook.

"I'd like to talk to my wife," he said.

"Sorry, she doesn't want to talk to you."

The man, who Kent knew to be Jim, took a step forward, putting Kent instantly on the defense. He definitely didn't want a fight, but he readied himself just in case. Jim reached into his back pocket, and before Kent knew it, he was yelling and shielding himself from a potential gunshot.

"Wait!" he yelled desperately. There was silence. He slowly lowered his hands that had been shielding his face, and looked expectantly at Jim, waiting to see the barrel of a gun. Instead, he saw a small white envelope which had been folded in Jim's back pocket, and when he opened his eyes fully, he realized that Jim was intending to hand it to him.

"Well then," he said tearfully, "will you give this to Kim for me, please?"

Kent realized then that he wasn't going to be shot, and stumbled over his words.

"Oh, yeah, of course. Sure man. No problem."

Jim handed the envelope to Kent and began walking back to his car. He stopped partway and turned back to Kent, who was still standing outside the front door.

"Hey man," he yelled, "I may have made some poor choices, eh, in my business, you know. But I'd never hurt anybody. Tell Kim I miss her."

Jim didn't wait for a response. He jumped in his car and closed the door. A few minutes later he was gone.

Kent went back inside as Kim came tiptoeing carefully out of the bedroom, where she had been listening to the entire exchange. She looked around, eyes searching Kent's for answers to unasked questions. Kent responded to her by handing her the envelope. Kim took it and sat down on the couch where she opened it slowly. She took out a check and held her other hand to her mouth, in utter shock. She was speechless.

From where Kent was standing, he couldn't tell what was in Kim's hand, and her expression didn't give away any details as to whether or not what was in the envelope was making her happy or scared. All he could infer was that whatever was in that envelope had shocked her.

Kent walked over slowly and gazed down at the paper that Kim was still holding in front of her. She hadn't moved her hand from her face nor the check from her lap. When Kent got close enough to where he could see it, he was able to make out a check, payable to Kim for two million dollars. He froze in shock too, not knowing what to say or do. Clearly, Jim had not come over in a jealous rage to threaten Kent as he had feared, but possibly as a husband who was trying to make things right after everything he'd put Kim through.

Kent continued to stare at the check, back at Kim, and back to the check again before he finally broke the spell that had frozen them both.

"Is there a note? Anything?" he asked.

Kim reached into the envelope and opened it up. Inside, there was, in fact, a small piece of paper that had been overlooked once Kim saw the check.

There was no explanation on the note, only the words:

"I'm sorry. Please take this money as my way of making things up to you. It is mine free and clear. There are no strings attached. Love, Jim."

This could only mean one thing, Kent decided. Jim would most likely be going away for a long time, and he wanted to do something to make things right with Kim before he did.

Kent sat down beside Kim and put his arm around her. She was crying now and leaned into him, letting the tears flow. She had so many mixed emotions for this man, this man that she had loved so much, who had yo-yoed her around in the last several weeks. He hadn't done it on purpose, but he had done it just the same and turned her world upside down. She was angry and grateful at the same time. She loved him and she hated him. She pitied him and she despised him.

He had gotten whatever he deserved, she decided...and then, wiping her tears as a small smile crept across her face as she looked at Kent, she decided she had gotten what she had deserved as well.

Chapter 45

Chapter 45

Now that she had a plan in place, Char thought there was only one thing left to do. She picked up her cell phone and dialed the one number that she used to call more than any other, but had resisted for the last several weeks. She took a deep breath as she nervously punched in the numbers on her cell phone, the numbers that reached directly to Kent's phone.

"Hi," he said.

"Hi." There was a pause. Char took another deep breath, willing herself to talk, despite wanting to hang up the phone and forget the idea entirely. But she knew she couldn't. She knew that in order to move forward, she needed to close the door on the past. Kent was her past, and Petra was her present, and hopefully would be her future. *Yes*, she said to herself, summoning her strength, *you can do this.*

Kent was just on the verge of hanging up the phone when she finally found the courage to speak.

"I, uh, how are you?" she managed.

"I'm okay, actually," he acknowledged. Surprisingly, he didn't sound angry. "And you? How have you been?" He sounded genuine.

Char let out a deep sigh. She was ready to share her truth with the man that she had once thought she would be with forever, even though she knew that things were better now...hopefully for both of them.

"I'm sorry, Kent," she managed. *Boy, that was hard.* "I, I thought I knew myself, but I didn't. It was never your fault," she said.

"I think I know," he said quietly.

"It wouldn't have been right," she needed him to know. "Kent, you provided me with a fabulous life. And I will always love you for it. But I need you to know, it wouldn't have been right for me to reap the rewards, the financial security, knowing how I felt. I couldn't help it, honest. Man, I would have done anything to feel more, more..." she paused, trying to find just the right words.

"Desire?" he suggested hesitantly.

"Yes, desire."

"And you feel that desire for Petra, I assume?"

"I believe so..." *God, this was hard.* "I mean, rather, yes, I do. And I wish I didn't, but I do. And you...you deserve so much more. You deserve someone who..."

"It's okay," Kent interrupted her. "You don't have to apologize. I should be the one apologizing to you."

Char thought painfully about that morning that would be forever imprinted in her memory, when she discovered her husband in bed with, with...it was too hard to say the words to herself, even now. But that didn't mean she didn't understand. She did. She got it. And truthfully, the mature side of her was just happy that he'd found someone. Not that she was surprised. He was still, after all, Dr. Dreamy. He was nice, kind, handsome, and well off financially. She knew he'd make the perfect husband again someday, for somebody, just not her, she realized. Char thought about everything she was giving up. A lot of women in her shoes wouldn't have had the courage to do what she did, to give everything up in exchange for a chance at true love. But then again, she smiled, she wasn't "every" woman. She was Char. She was Char who was now out and proud, who yes, was in love with another woman. A woman that she had never expected to fall for, for the sheer fact that she was, in fact, a woman. But now she knew. She understood what had been missing in her marriage, despite having been with the "perfect" guy. For Char, the perfect guy never would have been perfect for her, she realized.

She hung up the phone feeling at peace, having cleared the air with Kent. It was a time for new beginnings for them both. She hoped they would both be *better now...*

Back Matter

After moving up north to be with her friends and start a new life riding horses, Valerie gets dumped by her boyfriend, Duke, who was supposed to be joining her as soon as he could. Not only that, she falls off of her horse and winds up in the hospital...again. The only thing Valerie wants to do now is move back home to Southern California, where things were seemingly better before. It takes moving forward for Valerie to realize going backward isn't always the answer.

Find out what happens next in book three of the ***Never Say Forever*** series, **"*Better Before Than Forever*"**.

Never Say Forever series:

1. *Better Late Than Forever*

2. *Better Now Than Forever*

3. *Better Before Than Forever*

4. *Better Never Than Forever*

5. *Better After and Forever*

If you liked this book... please be so kind as to post a review! It helps new authors (like me!) to get my books out in front of readers. Or...

...Keep in touch! I can be found online at the following locations:
Website: https://shelleytan.com
Twitter: @shelleytan1
Facebook: Shelley Tan

shelleytanauthor@gmail.com and type **"newsletter signup"** in the subject line, to be sure to be notified of new releases and more information!